The Visitors Book

Also by Sophie Hannah

The Visitors Book

SOPHIE HANNAH

WITNESS
IMPULSE

An Imprint of HarperCollinsPublishers

Excerpt from *Closed Casket* copyright © 2016 by Agatha Christie Limited. Excerpt from *A Game for All the Family* copyright © 2015 by Sophie Hannah.

Originally published in 2015 by Sort Of Books, PO Box 18678, London, NW3 2FL.

EPub Edition NOVEMBER 2016 ISBN: 9780062562128

Print ISBN: 9780062669292

AM 10 9 8 7 6 5 4 3 2

The Visitors Book

I AM NOT a snob. My parents are snobs and so were my grandparents. Every member of my extended family apart from me is a snob, and I am nothing like any of them. I wasn't the one who bought a black cat with one white paw and named it 'Paw White Trash' – that was my cousin Lydia. She called it 'Trash' for short, and thought it was hilarious. My aunt Philippa commits the details of the *Sunday Times* Rich List to memory; I never even look at it.

And yet Aaron has just called me a snob. Which is ridiculous. Of the two of us, *he's* the snob. At the very least he's a pretentious idiot.

He's standing with his back to me, opening a bottle of wine. I shouldn't say anything. I should let it go. Except that, after what I've just discovered about him, I want to have the row more than I want this thing between me and Aaron to work. No doubt my desire to argue the point would pass if I gave it a chance – like a mosquito bite that stops itching if you can resist scratching it for long enough – but I lack the self-discipline.

'I might be a lot of things, but I'm not a snob,' I say.

When we got out of the cab last night and I saw his house for the first time, my reaction was entirely neutral. It was a house – no more and no less. I can honestly say that I had no thoughts about it at all. Only in the light of what happened later did it occur to me that Aaron's home is a two-up, two-down terrace on a street lined with similar houses, London brick on one side, white render dirtied to grey on the other. Aaron's is on the brick side.

What else did I notice? Washing hanging on lines in one or two front yards, net curtains to ward off nosy passers-by. Some clean cars, some dirty; one half collapsed, missing its front wheels. A man with a shaved head, wearing a puffa jacket and white trainers with huge, protruding tongues. But also . . . wasn't there an elderly man in an expensive suit and a long black overcoat? Yes, I'd swear there was. Now that I come to think of it, I nearly commented on it at the time, how bizarrely smart he looked. Christ, I'm glad I didn't. Aaron would be throwing it back at me now as proof of my snobbery: shock horror, a smartly dressed man on a down-at-heel street! But I'm not like that, really. When I saw Aaron's house I didn't think, *Oh dear, it's not a moated mansion.* Why would I? I didn't expect him to be landed gentry. He's an ordinary person, not an aristocrat, and that's fine.

'Snobbishness is my least favourite character trait,' Aaron says matter-of-factly now, as if he might not be talking about me.

'I'm *not* a snob,' I insist.

'When I asked you to sign the visitors book, you sniggered as if it was the most ludicrous thing in the world. "Flick to the end and add your name," I said.' Aaron smiles and hands me a glass of wine. 'You refused, and looked as if you were struggling not to laugh. Tell me what you found so funny and we'll see if there's snobbery involved.'

He doesn't sound angry. He sounds bored, as if it doesn't matter to him; he'd quite like to win the argument but he isn't emotionally invested in it. It makes me feel uneasy. So does the way he avoids my eye.

I stare down at the large green leatherbound book on the kitchen table. The visitors book: that's what he called it and that's what it appears to be. It has the words 'Visitors Book' on the cover in gold cursive writing.

'You could sign it now,' Aaron suggests. 'Why don't you, if only to make me happy? It might convince me you're not a snob.'

'Don't be ridiculous, Aaron. I don't need to prove anything.'

I can't work out why he cares so much about me signing his silly book.

I open it and start to flick through the pages, skimming the comments: 'Netterden is a fantastic house! We shall remember our visit with great fondness – The Flemings'; 'We had such fun and will take away with us plenty of memories to treasure – Winifred and John Santandreu, Islington, London'; 'The views from the terrace at dusk are breathtaking – Richard and Sue Graham'. Different inks, different handwritings. All are barely legible – shaky and erratic, as if the writers were sloshed, or too old and doddery to care.

The book appears to be genuine. How preposterous. I close it, not wanting to read any more nonsense.

'Are you seriously telling me that no-one else has found this book at all weird and been less than eager to sign it?' I ask, wondering if I'm the only person in Aaron's social circle who isn't deluded.

'So you're refusing, are you?' he says. His face is impassive. Since we met, I've been on the look out for signs that Aaron cares about me at all. He seems so remote – even when angry, as he is now. I'm physically close to him, but I feel as if he's miles away and there's a barrier between us that I'll never be able to get through. When we talk, I feel ignored. It's odd. And horrible. I ought to end it instead of hoping things will change.

'Have you never signed a visitors book before?' Aaron asks me.

'Yes. Some friends and I hired a manor house in Devon once, to celebrate finishing our degrees. Wortham Manor. It was several hundred years old – '

'Exactly the kind of place where you'd expect to find a visitors book,' Aaron cuts me off.

'I also . . .' I stop, realising that what I'm about to say might be taken as further evidence of my snobbishness.

'Go on.'

'One of my aunts is married to a lord – you know, in the House of Lords.'

'Well, I didn't think you meant a lord in the heavens above,' says Aaron.

I try to feel relieved at this rare sign of humour, but there was nothing warm about his joke. Somehow it made me feel even more alone. I read once in a women's magazine that being with the wrong partner, someone who doesn't understand you or who criticises you all the time, can be a lonelier experience than being single. I think it must be true, though I wouldn't have thought so before I got involved with Aaron.

'They've got a visitors book in their Hampshire house – my aunt and her husband,' I say. 'Well, it's a mansion, really.'

'Of course it is. And you signed their visitors book without almost bursting out laughing?'

'Credit me with some manners,' I say impatiently.

'Yet you were *so* tempted to laugh at me,' Aaron observes – again, apparently without emotion. 'And you refused, and still refuse, to sign my visitors book.'

I hate the way he speaks to me – as if I'm some sort of experiment he's in the middle of, not a fully fledged person in my own right. Now – this moment – is when I should tell him to fuck off and that I never want to see him again.

I can't leave yet. I'm too stubborn. I have to win this argument first.

'Aaron, you don't live in a mansion or a historical manor house. Those are the sorts of houses that have visitors books. Your house just . . . *isn't*. Look, is this a prank?

Did you forge all these different handwritings yourself when you were drunk one night? This is too ridiculous. I can't take it seriously.'

'You think I've got ideas above my station,' says Aaron. 'You're wrong.'

'It's not about above or below. It's . . .' I break off, frustrated. He *must* be able to see what I'm getting at.

'You're wrong,' he repeats.

'It's about context,' I try to explain. 'If I saw Prince Charles walking down the road wearing a babygro, I'd laugh and think he was an idiot. Whereas I wouldn't laugh if I saw a *baby* wearing a babygro! I don't think Prince Charles is worse, or less deserving of a babygro than a baby is. I'd laugh because it's a weird and surprising context in which to see a babygro, just as a two-bedroom terraced house belonging to a twenty-nine-year-old inner-city, secondary-school history teacher is an unusual context for a visitors book!'

'Mightn't a history teacher want to keep a record of the people who visit his home?' Aaron asks, sipping his wine. 'Think about it: *history*. Do you even know what year this house was built?'

It's the first good point he's made. For a second, I wonder if he's the sensible, open-minded one and I'm a bigoted fool. Then I come to my senses. 'Netterden,' I say. 'One of the comments in the book referred to the house as Netterden.'

'Really?' Aaron smiles. He nods at the book. 'Show me.'

'No! I've looked at it enough, thank you.'

'You don't want to touch it, do you? Why not?'

'Because it's so utterly absurd! I don't need to show you. It's your book – you must know its contents better than I do. I saw it, plain as day: *Netterden*. The name of your house, apparently. The Flemings think so, anyway, whoever they are. Whereas your front door seems to think it's called number thirty-two.'

'So it's pretentious to give a house a name?' Aaron asks. 'This from the woman who buys a car with the number plate LM04 LYX and immediately christens it Elmo Forelicks.'

'That's different,' I protest. Why do I feel as if he's winning? He isn't. He's plainly losing. Elmo Forelicks is not a name that anyone with delusions of grandeur would give their car.

'I bet your aunt's Hampshire mansion has a name, doesn't it? And you don't think there's anything wrong with that.'

'My aunt's house *needs* a name, for the simple reason that it isn't on a street. They could hardly call it 27, The Middle of a Load of Greenery, could they?'

Aaron closes his eyes. 'Will this argument ever end?' he murmurs.

'Would you prefer me to back down and say, "You're quite right, I'm so sorry"?'

'Yes, I would. And then I'd like you to sign my visitors book.'

'Jesus! Your obsession with getting me to sign that stupid book is bordering on the creepy, Aaron. Why does it matter so much to you?'

I won't sign it. I won't. No matter what.

'I'm the creepy one, am I?' Aaron laughs and shakes his head.

'You're suggesting I'm *creepy* for refusing to sign? No, sorry, that doesn't work. It's not logical. It's the wrong word. Intransigent, petty – possibly. Not creepy.'

'Like all snobs, you lack imagination. You can't think of *one single* hypothesis that would allow me to have a visitors book in my house and not be unbelievably pretentious, can you?'

'No, I can't. And I'm not sure I care any more.' I stand up, blinking back tears. 'I'm going home. Do you want to ring for the butler, or shall I show myself out?'

'Right.' Aaron chuckles. It sounds snide, as if he's mocking me in order to entertain someone else, but there's only us here. 'Because, while it would be acceptable for some people to have butlers – your aristocratic relations, for instance – it would be unthinkable for me to have one. Against the natural order of things, eh?'

'Fuck off, Aaron.'

I slam the front door behind me and march down the street without looking back. I have no idea where I'm going, where the nearest bus stop or tube station is. The wise thing to do at this point would be to banish Aaron from my mind entirely – all his stupid misconceptions and accusations – and be thankful I'm free of him, but I can't.

I don't feel free, neither of Aaron nor of the row we've just had. As I walk in no particular direction, I start up the debate again in my mind. Silently, I list all the excellent points I made and after each one I think, *Too bloody right! It shouldn't even need saying!* Arguing is so much more satisfying when your opponent isn't there to spoil your fun.

Netterden, for God's sake. Did Aaron decide to give his house that name, thinking a mere number wasn't good enough? I bet he did. I'm annoyed that I didn't think to ask him. If the house has been called Netterden for generations, why is there no sign on the door, the gate, anywhere? I'd bet everything I own that Aaron made up the name, aiming for something grand-sounding. Like Manderley, the house in Daphne du Maurier's *Rebecca*.

Last night I dreamed I went to Manderley again . . .

Manderley, in the novel, is a vast country estate. Would *Rebecca* have become a classic if Maxim de Winter had lived in a two-bedroom terrace in Walthamstow? No, it would not. Mrs Danvers would have had to sleep in the second bedroom, a stone's throw from the first; she'd have heard her boss and his new wife having sex through the thin partition wall.

All of this proves that I'm right and Aaron is either deeply pretentious or outright crazy. And who the hell are all his freakish friends who wrote those pompous comments in the book? I mean, were they just humouring him? They must have been. Or do they all also have two-bedroom houses with fancy names? The Flemings, Winifred and John Santandreu from Islington, London . . .

I stop walking.

Islington, London. Walthamstow, where Aaron lives, is also in London. Why wouldn't the Santandreus simply have written 'Islington'? Surely you wouldn't write 'Islington, London' unless you were writing in the visitors book of a house that was outside London. And . . . was there something else?

Yes. I'm sure of it. I saw something that really jarred in that awful visitors book, something I can't put my finger on. It's like a shadow snagging at the back of my mind. What was it?

I turn round to check Aaron hasn't followed me. There's no sign of him. I decide it's safe to stand here and allow myself to work it out.

Safe.

Since when have I been scared of him?

A woman passes me on the pavement. She smiles rather intrusively, as if to let me know I owe her a smile in return. She's wearing an expensive-looking coat over a red velvet dress, and high-heeled black shoes with gold and pearl buckles. Around her neck there's a string of pearls tied in a knot at the bottom.

Is it possible that Walthamstow is the new Chelsea and I've just not heard about it? Maybe everyone who lives here these days is a Russian oligarch, or related to one.

I look away. The smartly dressed woman looks as if she'd speak to me if I smiled at her, and I need to think.

I try to remember the other entries I read in Aaron's visitors book. There was one from a Richard and Sue something or other. 'Richard and Sue Graham', I think. 'The views from the terrace at dusk are breathtaking.'

Wait . . . is that it? Is that what I was trying to bring to mind a second ago, the detail that was wrong? It certainly strikes a false note. No one would say that about a terraced house. No one would call it 'the terrace' in that context. I am sure of this. Not Richard and Sue Graham; not anybody. They would say instead, 'The views from the *house* at dusk are breathtaking.'

Except they aren't. The view from Aaron's perfectly ordinary house, at dusk or at any other time, is nothing special, no matter which window you look out of.

Why didn't this occur to me before, when I first read those words in the visitors book? I was too busy skimming the pages for evidence of Aaron's pretentiousness. I must have seen 'terrace' and assumed that, since Aaron's house is a terrace, it made sense.

It doesn't. When you think carefully about it, it makes no sense at all.

I feel sick, and unsteady on my feet. I'm certain those words weren't written about the house I've just left. Richard and Sue Graham can't have meant Aaron's home. Wherever and whatever Netterden is, it isn't a terrace in Walthamstow; it *has* a terrace – with a stone balustrade and a fantastic view of the grounds. It's the sort of terrace where people might sit and sip champagne cocktails as the sun goes down. I can see it in my mind's eye, the whole scene. The real Netterden.

Why didn't Aaron tell me the truth? And, if Netterden isn't his house, why does he have its visitors book? Why did he try to insist I sign it, when he had no right whatsoever?

I close my eyes and go over exactly what happened when Aaron and I arrived at his house. The visitors book was on the kitchen table, closed. There was a pen next to it. I asked Aaron what the book was and he said, 'Isn't it obvious? It's a visitors book, as it says on the cover.' Then he ordered me – rather than asked me – to sign it. He very quickly called me a snob when I didn't comply, before I had time to focus on how strange it all was, how the comments couldn't possibly have been referring to the house I was in. Was Aaron gambling on being able to distract me, to make me focus on defending myself instead of on the oddness of the book and the words written inside it?

He told me no outright lies. He never explicitly said that his house was called Netterden. 'So it's pretentious to give a house a name?' were his exact words, and then he asked me if I couldn't think of another hypothesis to explain his having a visitors book.

I can now: he must have stolen it from the real Netterden. It shouldn't be too hard to find out. There can't be many houses with that name.

If only I had access to the internet. My phone's battery died some time ago. A library would do. How far am I from a library?

I've no idea, and I'm not calm enough to set about finding out. I fumble in my bag for my phone, shake it hard, then press the button to turn it on. 'Please, please,' I mutter, though I know it's pointless.

I don't believe in miracles even when they happen to me. There's always a catch. Yet my phone appears to have woken from its deep sleep. I'll need to be quick. The battery symbol's flashing red. I ring 118118.

When a woman answers, I ask for a number for Santandreu in Islington. I have to spell the name twice.

'I've got a Winifred Santandreu on Dunphy Road, Islington,' she says. It must be the right one. How many Winifred Santandreus can there be in London? I ask to be connected. A few seconds later, a man's voice says, 'Michael Santandreu speaking.'

'May I speak to Winifred?' I ask. 'Or John?'

'My parents passed away in January 2013,' he says abruptly. 'Who are you? Not a friend, I take it, if you didn't know.'

'My name's Victoria Scase. Look, I'm sorry, I'll leave you alone. It's not important.'

Silently I am thinking, *They both died in January 2013?* I can't decide if that's weird. Perhaps I'm the weird one and the rest of the world is normal. Come to think of it, I remember hearing something once about couples who've been married for many years dying within days or weeks of each other. Once one has gone, the other gives up on life and follows soon after. Perhaps that was what happened to Winifred and John Santandreu.

'What did you want?' Michael Santandreu's voice breaks into my thoughts.

'It doesn't matter.'

Why did I say that? It matters more than anything else in my world at the moment. I need to know what it was that Aaron didn't tell me. *Wouldn't tell me.*

'I might be able to help you with whatever it is,' Michael Santandreu offers, apparently keen to make me declare my business.

'I was just . . .' I clear my throat and start again. 'I was going to ask them if they remembered visiting a house called Netterden, but, as I said, it's really not . . .'

'Netterden?' He throws the word back at me like a stone.

'Yes. Why do you . . . I mean . . . You sound shocked.'

There's a long pause.

'That's where my parents were when they died,' Michael Santandreu says eventually. 'They were at Netterden.'

'Pardon?' I manage to say. The world tips on its axis. 'What . . . what *is* Netterden?'

'It's one of Gloucestershire's oldest houses. The Landmark Trust bought it about five years ago, to renovate. It used to belong to Penny and Clive Hoddy. That's where my parents died – at one of Penny and Clive's parties. Look, I'm sorry to be blunt, but if you don't know what happened in January 2013, why are you asking about Netterden? Who are you and what do you want?'

I can't speak. I try to ignore the thoughts drumming in the part of my mind I try so hard to avoid, but it's impossible.

How can I not know what happened at Netterden in January 2013? I used to know a lot, so why not now?

Meanwhile, other things, things I *am* sure of, I'm desperate to find a way to doubt.

Aaron's surname is Penny. His middle name is Clive. We laughed about it: 'Clive! What an awful name!' I blurted out.

Aaron Clive Penny. Penny and Clive Hoddy. I press my hand against a wall to steady myself.

To Michael Santandreu I say, 'Please, just . . . tell me what happened to your parents.' *But don't ask me to explain first. Hear my hollowed-out voice and understand that I need to know, straight away.*

They didn't die naturally, John and Winifred Santandreu. No. Not naturally at all.

How do you know that, Victoria Scase?

'Twenty-three people died that night,' Michael Santandreu says gruffly. 'Everybody there was killed. Murdered. My aunt and uncle too: Sarah and Peter Fleming.'

The Flemings. I know without needing to be told that Richard and Sue Graham are also dead.

'How? How did they die?' All on the same night, in January 2013 . . .

I gasp as a shadow at the back of my mind moves into the light.

That's it. That's the element that jarred, the detail I couldn't call to mind. There were no dates in the visitors book. It wasn't 'the terrace at dusk' – or rather, it was that as well, but it wasn't mainly that. It was the missing dates. Why weren't they there? People who sign visitors books always write the date.

Unless they know they're about to die. What does the date matter, on the last day of your life and if all of you, together, are signing the book on the same day? I think about the shaky handwriting, about how terror would make a person's hand shake more than alcohol or old age . . .

Murdered.

The comments they wrote . . . were they forced to come up with the wording themselves or did they have their entries dictated to them in a mocking tone? I shudder at the thought, then wonder where it came from.

Why can I hear the sneer in Aaron's voice so clearly?

'You haven't . . .' Michael Santandreu clears his throat. 'You didn't hear about it, on the news?'

'No. I don't watch the news, or read the papers, ever. Not since . . .' I stop, finding myself suddenly breathless.

Since what, Victoria Scase? It's Aaron's voice I can hear in my head. Why does he keep saying my name like that? I hate it. *Make it stop.*

I try to focus on my conversation with Michael Santandreu. 'What happened?' I ask him. It's all I can do to hold myself upright.

'They were shot – all the guests. Also the hosts, Penny and Clive, and their daughter Eleanor. I'm sorry, there's no nice way of putting it. The cleaner found the bodies the following Monday morning. Most of them had pens in their hands or lying near their bodies. I've no idea why, and the police couldn't make head nor tail of it. In a way, that remains the biggest mystery.'

'Who . . . ?' I start to ask, though I know the answer.

'Penny and Clive's son Aaron was and still is the only suspect. He disappeared that night and hasn't surfaced since. There was no break-in, you see.'

Pens in their hands.

'I met him once or twice,' says Michael Santandreu. 'There's absolutely no doubt in my mind that he did it.'

Nor in mine.

'That boy wasn't right in the head,' Santandreu goes on. 'He hated his family, thought his parents were appalling snobs. He must have decided mine were too, and all the other guests at Netterden that night. And his own sister.'

No. No. It can't be true. I'd have heard about it. People would have talked about it for weeks. Though I suppose I don't really speak to anyone any more, apart from Aaron.

Wouldn't the police have found him by now if they really believed he did it? I found him easily enough.

'You didn't sign the book,' a woman's voice says. It's coming from behind me. 'You wouldn't. You were the only one.'

I turn and see the woman in the red velvet dress that I saw before. She is holding her hand out to me as if beckoning me forward.

The woman in the red velvet dress isn't alone. There's a crowd of people behind her, all as smartly dressed as she is. Dresses, suits, ties. The man I saw on Aaron's street is one of them – the elderly one in the suit and smart coat.

Smartly dressed like me.

I look down at myself. I'm wearing a cream linen dress, pale pink high-heeled sandals, a pink and gold Missoni jacket. I wouldn't wear this outfit to come to Walthamstow, I'm sure.

The smartly dressed people are whispering to each other, 'She wouldn't sign the visitors book. Point blank refused. She was the only one.'

Because he was going to kill us all anyway, whether we signed or not. Couldn't you all see that? You should all have refused like me, you spineless saps.

The whispering stops. The smartly dressed ones stare at me as if they've overheard my thought.

'We were scared,' says Sue Graham. She rubs her hands together. There's ink on them. That's right, her pen leaked. I remember that.

I was there, at Netterden. All these people were there, and I was too.

Fuck you, Aaron. I won't sign it. Fuck you. Fuck y . . . And then silence. I remember.

'He's here, dear,' says Winifred Santandreu. She points past my shoulder.

I turn and see Aaron walking towards me. It's still light enough for me to see his face. He's holding the visitors book in one hand and a pen in the other.

The book itself is not supposed to visit, haha! The book is the host. It should stay at home. I might say this out loud if I weren't so scared. It will soon be over, I know, and I don't want it to be. I'll be forced to write 'Victoria Scase' in that wretched book, and then there'll be nothing else. Everything will disappear.

The book is the host.

I have to run, but I can't move. They're all around me, all the other guests, trapping me in the small space between them. All their mouths are moving, all their hands clutching and clasping.

'Sign it, Victoria,' Winifred Santandreu whispers. 'We all did. We'll help you.'

'Oh, yes, shall we? Do let's,' says her husband, John. 'Do let's help.'

'We need you, Victoria,' says Peter Fleming. 'We need your name. We must finish the book.'

Aaron moves closer. He turns the page. He holds out the pen.

I won't sign. I won't sign.

The Last Boy to Leave

WE ALWAYS HAVE Max's birthday party at our house, and the parents of his friends always tell us, as they drop off their children at the appointed time, how brave we are. Not brave at all, I say – simply not in favour of fun barns and soft-play centres and all other soulless party venues of that ilk, so what choice do we have? I'm not old-fashioned about many things, but I like the idea of my son celebrating his birthday in his home, surrounded by family and friends.

'We're going to have to go through it all again, you know,' I warned Greg an hour before the party was due to start.

He looked up from his newspaper. 'What?'

'The whole rather-you-than-me, aren't-you-brave rigmarole. People will think we're only doing it to show off our house.'

'But this is the first year we've had a big house,' said Greg. 'We did it when we lived in a two-bedroom flat.'

'Yes, but this lot won't know that. All the people coming are from Max's school – they've only known us since we moved here.'

My husband sighed. 'What do you want me to say, Jen? It's an insoluble problem. Why don't you hand out the phone numbers of some of our friends from Manchester? That way anyone who wants to can ring up and request proof that we hosted parties even when we were poor.'

He was right: what did it matter what people thought? It was wonderful to be able to do it properly this year. Instead of being crammed in and chaotic, we had all the rooms we needed. The magician – uninspiringly named Magical Steve – would be in the TV den with the boys. The girls would be in the dining room with Michelle the beautician, having intricate patterns painted on their finger- and toenails. I had laid out wine and snacks in the lounge for any grown-ups who wanted to stay, and Greg's and my bedroom had been designated the coat room. The playroom would be the venue for the children's party tea, and any presents people brought could pile up in the kitchen, where the goody bags were already waiting in neat rows. *All you need for a successful party,* I thought to myself proudly, *is a big enough house and good organisational skills.*

The doorbell rang. I looked at my watch. Ten past three. The party wasn't supposed to start until four. Greg went to answer the door. He reappeared a few seconds later looking alarmed. 'Magical Steve's here,' he hissed. 'What should I tell him?'

'He can set up in the TV den,' I said. 'It's fine. Offer him a cup of tea.'

Greg didn't seem to agree that it was fine. He groaned when the doorbell rang again at three fifteen. 'No one's supposed to arrive till four. This is going to be a nightmare. Can't you feel it slipping out of our grasp already? Party hasn't even started yet.'

I caught a glimpse of Magical Steve behind him, dragging a folded black-topped table into the hall, scratching the wallpaper. 'Don't exaggerate,' I said, determinedly smiling. What did Greg expect? That we'd open our front door on the dot of four o'clock and find all Max's classmates waiting in silence in jackets and bow ties?

The doorbell rang again at twenty past three and again at half past. I wasn't sure of the names of the early arrivals – Alex and Caleb were my best guesses; Max had only been at the school for a month – but they immediately began to run around the house emitting loud whoops. Max, at any rate, was pleased to see them, and immediately transformed himself into a savage in accordance with the time-honoured imitation-flattery model. Greg shouted, 'No need to make so much noise, boys!' Max had the grace to look sheepish but maybe-Alex and maybe-Caleb paid no attention. Their parents had vanished into the darkening winter afternoon. 'Did you invite them in?' I interrogated Greg. 'Did you tell them there was a buffet for parents upstairs?'

'No. They were gone before I had a chance to say anything.'

I stuck my head into the TV den to check on Magical Steve. He'd taken off his coat and was putting on a waistcoat: sparkly gold stars on shiny red fabric. There were large sweat stains on the armpits of his white shirt. I was about to offer him a drink when I heard a loud crash that sounded as if it had come from Max's bedroom. Two children's coats lay on the hall floor. I picked them up and threw them at Greg. 'Take these to the coat room. I'll go and persuade the boys to calm down.' My voice, I noticed, had taken on a desperate tone – the kind you hear in submarine disaster movies when the protagonists realise that water is pouring into the cabin.

The doorbell rang again. 'And while we're doing those things, who's going to answer the door?' asked Greg. 'This is going to be a – '

'Stop prophesying doom,' I cut him off before he could say 'nightmare'. 'Answer the door, then take the coats.' I was still kidding myself that we were in control – a pretence which, ten minutes later, I was forced to abandon. By quarter to four, everybody had arrived. The noise was unbearable. The house shook hard as twenty-five children ran up and down three staircases. Coats were strewn everywhere, as were crisps and sandwich contents; there had evidently been a raid on the party tea before it had been declared officially open. I had no idea how many parents, if any, were in the lounge helping themselves to wine. Every time I tried to go up there and have a look, I was sidetracked by one or other of the children I hardly recognised grabbing me and wailing, 'The boys tried to throw me off the bunk bed!' or 'Dominic bit me!' Who was Dominic? Was he the one with ADHD? Most of the party guests I'd encountered so far seemed to have ADHD or some other equally worrying condition.

I ran from floor to floor, hoping to catch a glimpse of Greg so that I could charge him with seizing control. I stopped every few seconds to hang a painting back on the wall, or scrape an embedded crisp off the carpet with my fingernails. How had crisps got up here, to the second floor?

The noise was getting worse; my house sounded like a packed football stadium. Over the general din, I heard Max howl, 'Mummee-eeee! Rufus is breaking my toys!' The doorbell rang. *Michelle, the nail woman*, I thought. Getting to the front door was out of the question. I was too far away and my son was still screaming. Magical Steve would have to let her in.

The rest of the party was a blur. I tried not to notice anything that happened, but a few highlights stood out, hard to miss: Greg running past me carrying a girl who was threatening to be sick under his arm, yelling, 'This will end, won't it? One day?'; a precocious girl called Arabella Hemming-Newman, whose name I did remember, sidling up to me as I wiped chocolate smears off the dining room wall and saying, 'Your house cost one million, one hundred and fifty pounds.' Shocked, I asked if Greg had told her that. 'No,' she said. 'Mummy looked it up on nethouseprices.com.'

Another girl asked why I'd arranged a magician for the boys and a beautician for the girls. 'I like magic and I'm a girl,' she said. I explained that Max had insisted: the girls had demanded professional nail action or else they wouldn't come to the party. Not this girl, apparently. She listened, nodding, then said, 'When I told my mummy, she said you're a throwback. What's a throwback?'

At ten to six, I started to carve up the cake, throwing pieces wrapped in napkins into goody bags. Parents began to ring the doorbell again. When they asked if I knew where their particular child was, I forced myself not to say, 'Oh, just take any. There are no individuals here. They've merged to form a rabble.' Two mothers contrived to devise a particularly exquisite form of torture; they left, with their children, then came back five minutes later. One had forgotten a grey hooded top, one a black scarf. 'Tell them to take whatever they want and go,' Greg muttered. 'The telly, the DVD player, our wallets – anything, as long as they leave.' The woman who had described me as a throwback insisted on being given a visitor parking permit, even though she intended to leave her car outside my house for less than a minute while she collected her daughter.

Finally, after the last stragglers had left, after we'd paid Magical Steve and Nails Michelle in cash and dispatched them into the night, I closed the front door and burst into tears. Max ran into the kitchen and started to rip the wrapping paper off his presents.

Greg, infuriatingly, seemed fine. 'It's over,' he yawned. 'Pour yourself a glass of wine and forget about it.'

I took him up on the first part of his suggestion. Armed with a drink, I made my way to the dining room, where I could sit and weep in peace.

'Mrs Rhodes?' said a quiet voice behind me.

I turned. A small dark-haired boy stood in the dining room doorway, goody bag in hand. 'When are my mummy and daddy going to come?' he asked.

I remembered him – not from school, but from earlier in the afternoon. He'd helped me to reassemble a broken Lego dinosaur in Max's bedroom. Later, I'd found him picking up flakes of tuna in the guest room, collecting them in his hand to take to the bin.

I didn't know his name, only that he was the one guest I hadn't at any point wanted to beat to a bloody pulp.

'Don't worry,' I said. 'I'm sure they'll be here soon.' *How odd*, I thought. I clearly remembered this boy and how helpful he'd been; I remembered rushing past the TV den and seeing him laughing uncontrollably at one of Magical Steve's tricks, and then thinking later, *I'm glad we put ourselves through this, if only for the sake of that one nice boy who seemed to enjoy the party so much.*

And yet, at the same time, my mind was full of memories that directly contradicted all of that: me dragging Greg into the loo on the ground floor and snarling at him, 'These children are vile – every single one of them. First thing tomorrow I'm looking into moving Max to a different school.' The nice helpful boy didn't seem to be part of that memory, or, rather, my awareness and appreciation of him wasn't. How could that be? And when I cut up the cake and considered spitting on each slice, why didn't I think to myself, *But I'd better put aside a clean piece for the helpful boy*?

I shivered. This was the weirdest feeling I'd ever had. It was as if I'd been two different women, at two different parties.

'Mrs Rhodes?' The boy's voice pulled me out of my trance. He was staring up at me, looking worried.

'Shall we go outside and look for your mummy?' I wiped my eyes and took him by the hand. 'What's her name?'

'Julia. My daddy's name is Tony. You've never met him, but Max's daddy knows him.'

'Do you know your home phone number?' As I asked the question, I heard ringing coming from the hall. 'Aha! I bet that's your parents,' I said to the boy. 'Come on. Let's go and see.'

Greg got to the phone before me. He looked worried as he listened. 'I see,' he said. 'That's . . . terrible.'

Oh, no, I thought. *Please not the nice boy's parents.* But . . . where was he? I couldn't see him anywhere. Where had he gone?

I ran out onto the street and nearly wept with relief when I saw the boy with a man and a woman. Each of them was holding one of his hands. 'Go back inside and find Mrs Rhodes, darling,' the woman said. 'Don't worry, there's nothing to be scared of. She's nice, isn't she?'

'Yes. Very,' said the boy. God, I liked this child. He could so easily have said, 'No, she's an irate harpy covered in crushed crisps.' I wasn't so happy about the 'go back inside' part. Then I realised that of course the boy's parents would insist he thanked me formally; these were people who knew how to raise a nice, non-repulsive child – the only ones in town, apparently.

But why 'go back inside', when I was outside standing right next to them on the pavement?

No, I wasn't. I was in the hall with Greg. How could that be? And the boy, once again, was nowhere in evidence. I heard his voice say, 'Mummy and Daddy have gone.'

'Jen.' Greg's voice sounded funny. I turned, saw tears in his eyes. 'That was Anne Garner on the phone. Anthony's mother.'

I had to think for a second. At first I thought he was talking about a mother belonging to one of our party guests, for those were the mothers I'd encountered most recently. Then I set myself straight. I'd never met Anthony Garner, but I knew the name well. He had been Greg's best friend all the way through school. He'd had an extensive collection of Tintin books, over which the two of them had bonded.

'Anthony and his wife Julia were killed two days ago. In South Africa. They've got a young kid Max's age – Oliver. I've never even met him.' Greg shook his head, angry suddenly. 'He wasn't with them, thank God. But . . . Christ, what's going to happen to him?'

Anthony Garner. Hadn't the boy told me his parents were Tony and Julia?

Oliver Garner. That was the boy's name. I felt . . . no, it was impossible. It couldn't be love. Whatever I felt for him, it couldn't be that.

'He must come here,' I said.

He's already been, I didn't say. *He's here now.*

Justified True Belief

THE SECOND THING I notice about the woman waiting to cross the road is that the roots of her teeth are visible and blackened where they meet the gum. I see them clearly as she talks: dark flashes in her pink mouth. She hasn't noticed that the green man is illuminated. Her friend has, but doesn't want to interrupt. Both are smartly dressed, with laminated name badges on strings round their necks. I can't read their names. The friend, the listener, is considerably more attractive. How could she not be, when the speaking woman is a ghost?

Which was the first thing I noticed about her.

They cross the street. The hem of the ghost's coat touches my car as she passes. Neither woman looks at me through the windscreen; I only realise I was afraid they would – afraid she would – once it hasn't happened. The green man gives way to the red. *You can go*, I tell myself, not moving.

I've seen a ghost. My body has turned to cold concrete. Other drivers, waiting behind me, beep their horns.

Somehow I manage to propel my car forward, swerving to the left, then too far to the right as I try to compensate. I turn down a side street and pull over. It's only once the car is still that I realise I'm shaking. What ought I to do? Tell someone? Even in my strange, frozen state, I am rational enough to know that there's no way to tell the story – and it's hardly a story; it was a few seconds at a zebra crossing, that's all – that will make it clear that the ghost I saw wasn't a perfectly ordinary, living and breathing woman with some kind of gum disease. She didn't behave in a frightening way, and she wasn't visible only to me; her friend saw her too, and heard her. 'How did you know she was a ghost?' people will ask me.

Because I did. Because of how I felt when I saw her. It wasn't fear. I didn't think she would harm me. Dread, horror . . . those words are more accurate. I would do anything to delete the memory of having seen her. Realising that this is impossible, I start to cry.

I was fine before I saw her – absolutely fine. My neck hurt a bit, but that is, unfortunately, normal for me. Just before the ghost appeared, I'd been thinking that today was a good day on the neck front, the best I'd had for a while.

The ghost's companion, crossing the road alongside her, definitely saw her. She was listening attentively, nodding her head. They were engaged in a conversation together. I don't believe the other woman knew that this wasn't a regular person she was talking to. The truth that was unmissable to me – from a greater distance and through a car windscreen – was invisible to her. Why?

I wipe the sweat from my forehead. I need to drive home, quickly, to prove to myself that I can get there. Seeing that . . . *thing* has left me feeling as if a windowless metal door has slammed shut, separating me from the rest of the world, the rest of my life. I'm in a sealed container and the air's running out.

You're in the car. Maybe that's the container you're thinking of?

I know it isn't, but I'm willing to try anything. I open the car door to the blustery day and inhale as deeply as I can. It makes no difference.

Will I tell anyone about this? Will I tell Rory, assuming I manage to get myself home at some point? The more people I tell, the more often I'll have to hear the words 'panic attack'; it's the easy and obvious thing to say, and it'll be said to me over and over again. No one will listen when I explain that panic doesn't come close to describing it. It's a heavy, slow feeling of being trapped in blankness – more like accounts I've read of clinical depression than anything terror-based.

She looked exactly like an ordinary woman: dyed auburn hair, greying at the roots; a small mascara smudge at the corner of one eye; a redness around her nose, perhaps from the wind. She didn't look like a ghost.

No matter how many times I say these words to myself, I am unpersuaded. I know I saw a ghost.

It's nearly an hour before I feel able to drive home. I see Rory through the kitchen window, a wooden spoon in his hand. The smell of lamb roasting reminds me why I went out – to buy a bottle of Merlot.

I don't want to go inside. Not because I've forgotten the wine but because I don't want to feel what I know I'll feel: that I'm in my house, but, at the same time, not there; that I'm with Rory, but not as much as the ghost is still with me.

The first thing I say to Rory is, 'You know I don't believe in ghosts.'

'Where's the wine?' he asks.

'I've just seen one.' I describe her as fully as I can – every detail I remember. 'She was crossing the road with a friend. Some teenagers were crossing in the opposite direction at the same time, but . . . no one else knew she was a ghost. No one apart from me. We all saw her – her friend saw her and heard her, and the teenagers . . . one of them swerved to avoid banging into her, but I was the only one who saw her for what she was.'

Rory grins. 'That's the worst excuse I've ever heard for forgetting to buy wine.'

'I'm not joking.'

'Well . . .' The curl of his mouth suggests the first stirrings of annoyance. 'That's unfortunate. Better to be joking than to have turned into a halfwit, I always think. And we still have no wine.'

I'd probably mock him if our roles were reversed. All the same, his reaction upsets me. Perhaps I ought to be more analytical: break this down into its constituent parts. 'You'd believe me if I told you I'd seen a woman with bad teeth – if that was all I said.'

'Ye-es,' Rory says slowly. 'Women with bad teeth – no problem at all. Give me a second and I'll try to pin down the part of the story that . . .'

'I can do without your sarcasm, Rory.'

'Hang on, I think I've got it. Yep, that's it: a *dead* woman with bad teeth strolling across the street – that's the part I have trouble with.'

'I have trouble with it, too. That doesn't change the fact that I knew she was a ghost the second I saw her.'

Arguing helps. Annoyance and frustration have started, slowly, to push the dread out of the way.

Rory shakes his head. 'This is crazier than your *Healing Hands* idea.'

'If by crazy you mean inexplicable, I agree. And *Healing Hands* wasn't crazy,' I can't resist adding. 'I might still contact them. There's no way their researchers aren't better diagnosticians than my GP. I know you lost interest in my bad neck when it lasted longer than a week . . .' I cut myself off with a sigh. This is an old argument. 'You haven't asked how I knew she was a ghost,' I say quietly. This conversation needs to be had, however much of an ordeal it might be.

'You can't know something that isn't the case, darling.' Still holding the spoon, Rory opens the oven with his other hand to check the lamb. 'You need to read up on the Gettier problem.'

'What's that?'

'A famous philosophical conundrum. Is justified true belief an adequate definition of knowledge? If it is, then we can say that S knows that G is true – S for Suzie, G for ghost – if and only if G is true, S believes G is true, and S is justified in her belief. Which . . .' – Rory slams the oven door shut with a smug smile – '. . . she ain't.'

'I don't know how I knew,' I tell him, ignoring his grandstanding. 'That's what scares me. Normally when someone asks you how you know something, you don't have to think about it. You know how you know, effortlessly.' I follow Rory around the kitchen as I speak, hovering behind him, not caring that I'm making him impatient. 'How do I know you're cooking lamb? I can smell it. How do I know you're finding me irritating? Your body language, your expression . . .'

'. . . the fact that you're *being* irritating,' Rory mutters. He sighs, turns to face me and says, 'Can you keep an eye on the lamb while I nip out to the off-licence for wine?'

———

FIVE WEEKS LATER, after I have allowed Rory, the philosopher Edmund Gettier and common sense to convince me that I was wrong, I see another ghost. This time it's a young man with a ponytail, in front of me in the queue at the post office. He's holding a rigid A4 envelope, the words 'Handle With Care' printed on it in red.

I have no idea how I know he is a ghost, but there is no doubt in my mind, even though I cannot see his face. Once again, fear freezes me. This time it's more convenient, because I'm in a queue that's not moving. I remind myself that I don't believe in the supernatural, but it has no effect. That opinion, one I've expressed so often and with such certainty, now feels like a discarded fancy-dress costume – silly and irrelevant.

Ask him. 'Excuse me – you're not dead, are you, by any chance?' I know what Rory would say, once he'd stopped mocking and/or shouting at me not to be stupid: anxiety about the trapped nerve in my neck, or whatever it is, has made me more susceptible to morbid thoughts, and the constant pain isn't helping.

I tap the young man on the shoulder. When he turns, I say, 'Look, this is going to sound odd, but . . . can you tell me something about yourself? Anything. What's your name? What do you do?'

He seems taken aback, keen to put as much distance as he can between himself and me. Has no woman ever spoken to him unprompted before? How strange. He looks like a frightened mouse.

I don't care if he thinks I'm a lunatic. Whatever he says, even if it's 'Get lost, freak', I will feel better. I need him to demonstrate that he's firmly anchored in the real world.

He says nothing. 'Please,' I say. 'Please answer.'

'Why?' He stumbles over the word, though it's a simple one. 'Do you recognise me from somewhere'?'

'Maybe,' I lie.

'My name's Dermot. I'm twenty-seven, I'm a welder. I have a girlfriend. We . . . we live together.'

Does he think I'm trying to pick him up? *He's saying all the wrong things.*

'Tell me the most important thing,' I whisper, my heart hammering. How did I know to say that? How do I know there's something more important than what he's told me already? I don't have justified true belief. All the same, I believe Dermot has something crucial to tell me.

He looks angry. Trapped. 'I've got a brain aneurysm,' he says eventually. 'There's a good chance it's going to kill me. How did you know?'

LATER, I EXPLAIN to Rory how the puzzle fits together. The welder, Dermot, has a life-threatening condition. The woman at the zebra crossing looked unhealthy; her black tooth situation might be the result of gum disease, or even something more serious. My neck's been plaguing me for two months – of course I'm going to be sensitive to other people's pain. There's nothing supernatural about it. When Rory goes to bed, I'll do some research on the internet.

ONE OF THE more interesting results that comes up when I type 'sore neck' into the search box is a website called Spirit Harmony. It's the online home of a guru based in Bloomington, Indiana. There's a page on her site that matches common physical ailments to their correct spiritual diagnoses. For sore neck she's got: 'Sometimes, pain in the shoulders and especially in the neck is a sign that you are ready to embark upon a period of significant spiritual growth. Do not deny the message your body is sending you. Instead, allow yourself to step into your own abundant spiritual potential, and inhabit it fully.'

I have no idea what this means. It's made my neck hurt more. I wish there were a way of leaving a comment on the website. Didn't the guru stop to think that some people reading her advice might be married to men like Rory? If I told him I wanted to find a way to inhabit my own abundant spiritual potential, he'd probably say something like, 'Yes, but can we get the new kitchen sorted out first?'

I type 'brain aneurysm' into the search box. It's the only solid lead I have. As the results fill my computer screen, I wonder if I'm going about this the wrong way. Solid leads, traditionally, help people to catch flesh-and-blood criminals, not ghosts.

DR CAROLINE SIMM is the UK's leading brain aneurysm expert. I'm lucky to get an appointment with her at such short notice. She is running nearly two hours late. I sit in her waiting room with three other people, one of whom – an elderly man – is a ghost. I can't stop staring at him, though the sight of him fills me with dread.

I should turn away. He's shooting nervous glances in my direction every few seconds; each time he looks, he finds me staring at him. He shudders as he catches my eye, as if afraid I might be about to pounce on him. I am trying to be subtle, to watch him without him noticing; clearly it's not working.

He's not a ghost, I tell myself firmly. *He has a brain aneurysm, like Dermot – that's why he's here to see Dr Simm.*

My little pep talk makes no difference to how I feel. I still know the man is a ghost. I don't know how I know.

Ten minutes later, I am telling Dr Simm about my neck. 'My GP insists it's a trapped nerve that'll come free at some point, but I've had trapped nerves before – it's a different kind of pain. I've seen locums, been to A&E – no one could come up with anything else it might be. I got so desperate, I nearly contacted *Healing Hands*.' I laugh as if embarrassed, pretending to think my good idea is a bad idea.

Dr Simm looks puzzled.

'You know, the TV drama?'

She plainly doesn't know.

'Every episode, someone's got some bizarre combination of symptoms, and these brilliant doctors work out what's wrong just in time to save their life.'

Why am I telling her this?

'Look, I know what's wrong with me, and I need you to save me. Nuchal rigidity.' I sound like someone who's been Googling. 'I have a brain aneurysm. Scan me. You'll see I'm right.'

Dr Simm smiles indulgently. 'A trapped nerve is far more likely in a healthy young woman like you.'

I tell her she's wrong. Then I take a deep breath and tell her that I've been seeing ghosts or, rather, seeing people with brain aneurysms and perceiving them as ghosts. Three fellow sufferers, so far. Gum disease with blackened tooth roots isn't a symptom of brain aneurysm; the woman I saw at the zebra crossing must have had both. It happens often on *Healing Hands*: a patient presents with two unrelated symptoms. One is caused by something lethal but curable if caught in time; the dramatic function of the other is to impede correct diagnosis until precisely fifty minutes into the programme, leaving ten minutes at the end for life-saving.

'Dr Simm, there's no doubt in my mind that I've been . . . led to this awareness of what's wrong with me. Whenever I see someone with a brain aneurysm – a living person – *I see them and perceive them, as a ghost.* Even though they're not dead!'

Yet.

I don't bother to recite my speech about knowing without knowing how I know. What's the point? It's never going to satisfy anyone but me. It's not logical.

'I believe I've been *shown* this truth because I need urgent medical treatment to save my life – treatment for a brain aneurysm. I need you to give me that treatment.'

'So your theory is . . . what? That you yourself have this condition, and you therefore see others with the same condition as ghosts for that reason? Some kind of . . . intuitive link between people suffering from the same problem?'

'Yes, exactly.' Thank God. She gets it.

'Then why don't they see you as a ghost? Why doesn't it work both ways?'

'I don't know! Maybe it's just . . .' I stop, open-mouthed. 'No, that's wrong. They *do*. They *do* see me as a ghost. Dermot the welder, and the man in your waiting room . . . they looked terrified when they saw me, when I spoke to them. And the woman crossing the road didn't look in my direction. I was in my car. Pedestrians don't see beyond the car, usually, to the person or people inside it.'

If she'd seen me, she'd have screamed. I know she would.

Dr Simm nods. 'And the man in my waiting room now – he's one of these three ghosts that you've seen?'

'Yes.'

'And the two women?' She glances down at her appointments diary, which lies open on her desk, and frowns. 'Aren't there two women out there, as well?'

'Yes, but . . .'

'They weren't ghosts?'

'No.'

'Then your theory falls down.' Dr Simm smiles. 'Both those women have intracranial aneurysms.'

But they weren't ghosts. Definitely not.

'There's a difference,' I hear myself say. I don't want to ask, but I can't stop the words coming out.

You don't need to ask. You know.

That's true. But how, for God's sake? How do I know?

'What's the difference between the two women and the man?' I ask, struggling for breath.

After a pause, Dr Simm says, 'His aneurysm's in a more dangerous position. It's more likely to kill him. Brain aneurysms are sometimes, though not always, fatal.'

The two women in the waiting room saw me and showed no sign of fear or aversion.

'The ghosts are the ones who are going to die of the same thing that's going to kill me,' I say, as dread spreads through my body. 'A brain aneurysm. We see each other as ghosts, though no one else sees us that way.'

Is this what fully inhabiting my spiritual potential means? Becoming a ghost, becoming dead?

Dying. Dying, dying, dying.

'This is ridiculous,' I say, trying to laugh. 'I'm talking rubbish, aren't I? Dr Simm? Why don't you tell me I'm talking rubbish?'

*All the Dead Mothers of
My Daughter's Friends*

I FEEL SICK when I see Grace Taggart waving the shiny gold envelope in the air. 'I got it again!' she yells across the playground with a little hip wiggle before running towards her mother. Now I know why my daughter Bee is walking so slowly – at the back of the crowd, head down.

'Fucking great,' I mutter under my breath.

'What's great?' a clear voice beside me says. I turn and see a woman I haven't noticed before. Her hair looks flammable: thick, straw-like, dark blonde.

'That's wonderful, darling!' Rachel Taggart calls out to her daughter. To the mother on her right, she says, 'God, this is embarrassing. Some children haven't won it at all, and Gracie keeps winning it. But, I mean, what can I do? I have to be pleased for her, don't I?'

'Oh, I get it,' Straw Woman lowers her voice beside me. 'You're annoyed Bee didn't get Star of the Week.'

And that someone I've never laid eyes on before knows my daughter's name.

I nod. Too upset to be diplomatic, I say, 'I fucking hate Star of the Week. All it does is create twenty-one non-stars every week in each class, some of whom, like Bee, have never won it. Grace Taggart wins it literally every other week.' I want to know who I'm talking to before I say any more. 'Are you ... Do you have ...?'

'Lisa Paskin.' She holds out her hand. I shake it. 'I'm Harriet's mother. She's new in Bee's class.'

'Oh.' Shit. I ought to know the name, in that case. Harriet Paskin, Harriet Paskin. Right, that's in my memory now. 'Good to meet you. Bee's newish too – start of last term. She'll never win Star of the Week; she's too rude to the teachers. It's my fault. She's inherited my loathing for authority figures. Last week Mr Orton made a joke in front of the whole class about Bee hating science – I mean, she does hate it, but even she can see that he ought to try to help her to like it more, not enshrine her hatred of it in class legend. What was I saying? Oh yes ... so he said that, and everyone laughed, and Bee just turned very calmly to face him and said, "Sir, when you were my age, did you always dream of being a supply teacher?" Apparently his mouth actually dropped open in shock, and the class laughed more at her joke than at his. I tried to be angry when she told me, but secretly I was thinking, *Hah! Nice one, Bee.* But I did point out that, with an attitude like that, she can hardly expect to win Star of the Week. The thing is, she does. It's like she thinks the award's given in recognition of great dialogue, not good old-fashioned proper behaviour.'

Bee and her friends have stopped halfway across the playground. Some of the girls are chatting frantically, but I can see Bee's not really engaged. She looks over at me, signalling with her eyes that she'd like to get out of here as soon as possible, but she has to go through the motions if she wants to fit in. So far, she's popular in her class. She's the Fearless Backchatter – that's why she can't stop being rude to teachers. None of her friends would guess that she'd love to be Star of the Week. She'd be nonchalant, even dismissive, if she got it, but that doesn't mean she doesn't want it.

'If it's any consolation, Harriet would give Bee her Star of the Week award every week,' says Lisa Paskin. 'I would, too. Thanks to Bee, they learned about perspective in Art this week, and light and shade. That wouldn't have happened without her . . .' Lisa stops and claps a hand over her mouth. 'Oops. I might have put my foot in it. I assumed . . .'

'Don't worry, Bee told me about her, um, intervention. And again, subversive monster that I am, I was on her side. I mean, it's Art! Fucking Art, and they propose to devote the whole of term one to making hats?'

'"That's not art, it's millinery. Did Leonardo da Vinci start his art career by learning to make a felt hat?"' Lisa quotes my stroppy daughter. 'Brilliant!'

I can't help smiling proudly. 'She followed that up by writing and handing in a list of everything the Art teacher ought to be teaching them but wasn't, starting with a breakdown of all the different sorts of pencils and which kind to use for what type of drawing. Again: my fault. She wouldn't have known what to put on that list if she hadn't spent hours listening to me and her artist father bitching over the dinner table.'

'She's great, Mel. Seriously. Who cares about a stupid certificate? Your Bee's a real star.'

'Yeah. Trouble is, she won't see it that way. She's in a bind – a natural rebel who nevertheless wants approval. But won't lift a finger to get it.' I sigh. I'm trying hard to like Lisa Paskin – I ought to like her, in the light of her strong support for Bee – but I find it unnerving that she knows so much about me and my family. She knew my name was Mel. How? I haven't introduced myself to her.

'Anyway, I think you'll find Grace Taggart hasn't won Star of the Week, though she evidently believes she has,' Lisa says with an enigmatic smile.

What's she talking about? 'No, she's won it. Look, she's brandishing the gold envelope. Her adoring acolytes have gathered round to shower her with congratulations. Yes, I am being bitchy about an eleven-year-old. I can't help it. Have you seen her Instagram account? Her user name's "babybeautiful". I mean, ugh. Every single photo she posts is of her, pouting like a Botoxed goldfish.'

Lisa laughs. 'What do you expect? You know her mother buys her new clothes every day, practically? Dresses her up like a doll.'

'Ssh, keep your voice down. She'll hear you.'

'She wouldn't bother listening to the likes of you and me. She has no interests apart from Grace, her Baby Beautiful – you know that's where Grace's Instagram username came from, right?'

I shake my head. How does Lisa know so much? Perhaps she doesn't do her best to stand fourteen miles away from the other mothers at pick-up time, like I do. I'm sure some of them are lovely and fascinating – just not the ones I've met.

'Rachel Airhead Taggart doesn't even have her own email address,' Lisa sneers. 'All her jolly round-robin emails to us lesser mothers, entitled "Long-Overdue Mums' Night Out!", come from her husband's email.'

'I know. GRAHAM TAGGART, all upper case. That's how I think of her. In my mind she's not Rachel, she's GRAHAM TAGGART in Caps Lock.'

'If there's one thing worse than this school, it's the mothers at the gates. Not you, Mel – you're the exception, which is the only reason I'm talking to you.'

This woman is nasty, I can't help thinking. Worryingly, though, she's said nothing that I haven't thought many times myself. Maybe I'm equally nasty.

'But the others, Jesus wept! They're appalling. That one over there with the auburn bob, in those hideous half-leggings, half-jeans things – her name's Julie Laycock.'

I know that, Lisa. Bee has been at the school longer than Harriet.

Which among the dishevelled uniforms in the playground is Harriet Paskin? I've memorised her name but I have no idea what she looks like, this fan of Bee's. I wonder if she's nicer than her mother.

'Julie invited me round to hers for coffee when we first met, and then spent two hours complaining about her husband,' Lisa tells me. 'Whenever he buys her a present, apparently, it's always something he wants himself, but he pretends it's something he thinks she'd really like. I made the mistake of asking her if she did like some of the presents. She made a disgusted face and said, "Even if I liked the things themselves, I'd never give him the satisfaction of admitting it. They've all gone straight in the bin. He has to learn." I can't imagine why he stays with her, unless he's equally awful.'

'He is,' I can't help saying. 'Both times I've met him, he's found an opportunity to tell me his Life Motto. Oh, yes, he has one – an official one: "I don't live to work, I work to live."'

'Ha! I'm sure he works mainly to avoid his reptile of a wife!' Lisa giggles. 'I used to think Jenny Buckley was okay – dark, ponytail, bright-green coat – but then there was the baby name thing. You know she's preggers?'

I nod.

'I asked her what she was planning to call the baby and she said Fred. They know it's a boy. I laughed, assuming she was joking and said, "Yeah, right. What are you going to call it, really?"'

'Why shouldn't she call it Fred?'

'Because her daughter, in Harriet and Bee's class, is called Rose.'

Bee and Harriet's class, actually. Bee was there first.

Ugh, get over yourself, Mel. You're being pathetic.

'Fred and Rose! The Wests! World-famous serial killers!' Lisa shakes her head. 'I felt obliged to tell her, thinking she'd obviously want to think twice before naming her children after a pair of rapist-murderers, but she said, completely straight-faced, "My grandparents' names were Fred and Rose. That's who I'm calling my kids after, not the Wests." She said she didn't think anyone would remember the Wests in a few years time anyway. How deluded can you get?'

'Yes. One might not think of the West connection oneself, but once it's pointed out . . .'

'And then there's the revolting Suzanne Fox! She's the worst of the lot. The other day she was wittering about how she's going to make sure Ethan always spends Christmas Day with her, for the rest of his life. She's happy to have his future wife and her entire family to stay for Christmas, she says, but she won't allow Ethan, ever, to spend a single Christmas Day away from her. "Allow" – that was the word she used. The boy's eleven, for Christ's sake, and she's making Christmas plans for his hypothetical future wife's parents. How mental can you get?'

'I think Anna Gimblett might be okay,' I say. 'The one with the wide face and long blonde hair.'

'Yeah, I know her. I thought the same at first – that she was all right – until she started talking to me about ghosts.'

'Ghosts?'

'Yup. She started in the usual way: she's not the sort of person who believes in any of that nonsense, but . . . and then some ridiculous story about waking up in the middle of the night and feeling a presence, blah, blah. It's always the middle of the night, isn't it? And the person telling the story is always a perfectly rational atheist who had no truck with the supernatural, until. I mean, no one ever says, "I'm precisely the sort of suggestible idiot who'd believe anything, so really I wasn't surprised at all when a ghost selected me as its audience." Hey!' Lisa grabs my arm, as if she's just remembered something exciting. 'Are you going to the Mums' Night Out tomorrow?'

'I think so,' I say. 'Not that I want to, but I missed the last one. GRAHAM TAGGART has made it clear, in that deadly light-hearted way of hers, that all the mums expect me to be there this time. Two consecutive absences . . . well, let's just say there would be consequences. Why, are you going?' I ask Lisa.

'Not a chance. I've got better things to do. But . . . I don't suppose you could do me a favour, could you? Anna "Ghosts" Gimblett annoyed me so much, I decided to try and out-ghost her. I fed her some bullshit about the difference between ghosts you see at night and the ones you see in the daytime. She didn't believe me, I don't think, but . . . it'd be hilarious if you told her the same story. The more people she hears it from, the more she'll start to wonder if it might be true. She might start telling other people. Fancy playing Torment the Credulous Cretin with me?'

No, I don't. I don't want to be assigned a stupid chore by Lisa Paskin. I'm curious, however. 'What did you tell Anna about the difference between night ghosts and day ghosts?'

Before she has a chance to answer, there's a piercing howl. I turn and see that Grace Taggart is sobbing, her face red and wet. The gold envelope lies by her feet, torn in half. In her hand, she's holding her Star of the Week certificate, but she's . . .

Can she be tearing it up?

'What the hell?' I stare in disbelief as the fragments fall to the ground.

'Mumm-yyyy!' she screams. Most of the girls in Bee's class say 'Mum', but not Grace. I once heard Rachel say to Suzanne Fox about her son Ethan (he of the preemptively restricted Christmases), 'Aren't you devastated that he's stopped calling you "Mummy"? I've told Gracie I want to be "Mummy" forever!'

Rachel Taggart hurries towards her Baby Beautiful. I try not to be happy that a child is unhappy. It's hard. For as long as she's been Bee's so-called friend, she's done everything she can to undermine Bee's confidence. In our house, we have a Classic Grace Taggart Comments Collection. Our favourite so far is: 'You're pretty, Bee, but you're not beautiful like me. I'm not being big-headed, I'm just confident. That's a good thing. You should try to be more confident. Confidence makes you more attractive.'

Bee isn't allowed to buy clothes from Ballihoo because that's where Grace buys her clothes. Bee isn't allowed to wear white nail varnish because that's Grace's favourite colour, or part her hair on the left because Grace does that. All of these rules Bee grudgingly accepts, instead of telling Grace to set fire to her head and stick it up her arse, as I've suggested on many occasions.

'Oh, my God! Oh, my God!' Rachel Taggart is holding up the pieces of the torn-up certificate. 'This is monstrous. Look at this! Who's done this? Who's done it? You'd better tell me right now, whoever you are!' Mothers are hurrying towards her to see what's the matter.

'We'd better go over, I suppose,' I say to Lisa.

'Why? So that we'll look like we care? I couldn't give less of a shit if I tried. Grace Taggart's a vile little bitch.'

'Basic curiosity?' I suggest. 'I want to find out what's going on.' This is absurd. I don't need Lisa Paskin's permission to show an interest.

'I can tell you what's going on: Grace opened her gold envelope, thinking she knew what she'd find inside it, and instead she found something superficially similar but substantively different: a Bitch of the Week certificate.' Lisa smiles. 'Of course, the big mystery is: how and when was the switch done? And by whom?'

'How do you . . . ? *You*? You did it? You put a certificate saying "Bitch of the Week: Grace Taggart" in that envelope?'

'Not personally.' Lisa winks at me. 'I might have arranged for it to be done.'

'Fuck, Lisa. How did you arrange it? Aren't you worried about getting booted out of the school if they find out?'

'You mean, aren't I worried about Harriet getting booted out? I'm not a pupil here myself. No, I'm not worried – about that or anything. I never worry. Besides, anyone who gets booted out of this school's lucky. You know what Bee and Harriet did in their most recent PSHE lesson? Did Bee tell you?'

'No, I . . . No. I don't think she did.' I'm finding it hard to concentrate on Lisa, with Rachel and Grace Taggart both weeping a few metres away, and other mums and girls crowding round to comfort them.

'The subject was racism.' Lisa's face hardens as she speaks. 'The message was the obvious and correct one: racism's terrible. Guess how that message was conveyed? A video was shown to the class of a group of racist thugs racially insulting a black person on the tube. The class was actually made to watch the film of racist abuse! They were made to watch it happening, as if they were there watching it live! Guess how many black kids there are in Harriet's class? One! Only one. And that poor girl had to sit and watch this film of horrible racist invective.'

'That is . . . bad,' I agree.

'If you ask me, that teacher should be fired! If they'd shown them, I don't know, *To Kill a Mockingbird* or *Cry Freedom* – a movie that contains racism but also the condemnation of it, with the non-racist characters clearly shown as the goodies – that would be completely different. But just a video of extremely distressing racist abuse? An immersive racism experience for all the eleven-year-olds? The black girl, Ellie, started crying – as you would. All the other kids had to hug her to cheer her up, while the teacher, from what I can tell, did sod all. Sat back and did not hug. I mean, could he not think of any better way to make the point that racism is bad? Could he not have dug up some old footage of Stevie Wonder and Paul McCartney singing "Ebony and Ivory"? What's on the syllabus for next week: an Auschwitz gas chambers installation in the classroom? Jesus Christ, this school!'

THE MUMS' NIGHT Out is at the Shezan, an unpretentious Indian restaurant with an all-you-can-eat buffet. In spite of this, the mums are dressed as if for the Oscars, in strappy shiny dresses and high heels. I'm wearing jeans, pumps, a checked shirt. I've made sure to sit next to Anna Gimblett in case I decide to resort to the supernatural.

It turns out that I might want to do Lisa Paskin a favour after all. After her 'Bitch of the Week' coup, I can't help but be favourably disposed towards her. Impressed, too. How the hell did she pull off the Bitch Switch? I would love to know.

Julie Laycock is talking about death. 'I told Maisie and Izzie yesterday: when our time comes, Mark and I have decided we want to be buried, not cremated, so they'll have to sort that out for us.'

Can that time please be soon? Like, before anyone suggests staying for dessert and coffee? Sitting next to Anna meant getting stuck at the very end of the table with only her, Julie Laycock and Jenny Buckley for company. Oh, fun times.

'It made sense to tell them, I thought,' Julie goes on. 'We were updating our wills. Mark and I don't think there should be anything a close family can't discuss. I did apologise to the girls, because obviously burial means more hassle for them once we're dead and gone, but I do find it comforting, the idea of having a resting place. Mark does too, now. I talked him round.'

'Why more hassle?' I ask.

'Pardon?' Julie blinks at me. It's the first thing I've said to her all evening, or she to me. I've hardly spoken since I arrived, apart from the obligatory how-are-yous.

'I can't see why having your parents buried is any more laborious than having them cremated,' I say. 'Either way you need to organise the event, whatever it is, and have a funeral and all that stuff.'

Julie sighs heavily. 'Don't be thick, Mel. With cremation, the ashes are scattered and that's it, job done. With burial, there's a grave to be visited and tended week after week, year after year. There's a . . . a site that needs to be maintained.'

Did I hear a note of pride in Julie's voice? Is she actively looking forward to being a high-maintenance cadaver?

'Don't the church gardening staff do that?' Jenny Buckley asks.

'Oh, no, it's the family that looks after the grave,' Julie tells her. 'Absolutely. Think of the weeds growing all over it. It can start to look messy very quickly. Plus, a kind of competitive thing kicks in – other families make their loved ones' graves look spectacular and no one wants to seem a slacker in front of those people, do they?'

'I keep wondering . . .' Driana Roberts leans over and cuts in, '. . . is it okay that we're here, going ahead with our night out as planned, while poor old Rachel's miserable at home? She was the one who did all the organising. It doesn't seem right.'

'She should have come,' says Julie Laycock. 'I told her: come along and show whoever did it that you're not intimidated. I mean, she must know none of us would do a thing like that. It makes no sense, anyway. A person who gives a child a Bitch of the Week certificate is self-evidently a bitch themselves, as proven by their own actions.'

Why don't they suspect Lisa? I wait for one of them to mention her, but no one does.

Come to think of it, why don't they suspect me? I'd totally have done it if I'd a) thought of it, and b) seen a detection-proof way to do it.

'Poor Grace,' Anna Gimblett sighs.

'Maybe Mrs Harkness did it,' I suggest.

'Don't be ridiculous,' says Julie. 'What form teacher would do that? Whoever did it's got a screw loose. Grace is lovely. I mean, yes, she does seem to feel the need to overshadow the other girls, and she puts herself forward way too much, but she's learned that from Rachel – you can't blame the child. Not that I'm blaming Rachel, I just meant . . . well, you know.'

'Returning to the subject of your death, Julie,' I say. 'I'd go for cremation if I were you and Mark. Burial's a hostage to fortune. What if your kids don't bother to tend your grave, or even visit? You know where you are with cremation: once you're scattered, you're scattered. I suppose they might not bother doing that either, but personally I think they're more likely to. A scattering's a one-off – most people would make the effort.'

Julie's eyes widen as her lips narrow. 'You're suggesting that my daughters might not bother to look after their own mother's grave?'

'Who knows?' I grin at her. 'People are busy. Do you have spare time for grave-tending? I don't. Maybe Maisie and Izzie won't. Or maybe they'll find it too upsetting to go, or they might secretly resent you and use the non-maintenance of your grave as a way of showing it once you're safely out of the way, if they're too scared to stand up for themselves now.'

I know for a fact that Izzie Laycock, at least, is ter-rified of her mother. She's not allowed to watch *Pretty Little Liars* at home, and when Bee suggested they watch it at our house and there was no way Julie would find out, Izzie nearly started crying. 'I'd have to tell her myself,' she said. 'We have a rule in our family – we tell each other everything.'

Julie Laycock is, I believe, a practitioner of Covert-Reign-of-Terror parenting, the sort that kids don't realise they've had until they're in their mid-thirties at least. Julie's chosen burial over cremation because it pisses her off to think that after her death she won't be able to emo-tionally blackmail her daughters any more. *How can I still make them do stuff for me from beyond the grave?* will undoubtedly have been part of her thought process. No doubt she'll stipulate that her gravestone must be hewn from a rare granite that needs polishing every Tuesday at exactly quarter past three in the morning.

If you want to end up with your epitaph obscured by weeds, Covert-Reign-of-Terror parenting is the way to go. I wish Lisa Paskin were here – she'd agree with me, I'm sure.

'I'd totally haunt my girls if they didn't take proper care of my grave,' Julie smiles around the table at every-one but me, trying to lighten the mood. 'I'd appear at the foot of their beds every night and give them a thorough ticking-off!'

It's the perfect opportunity. How can I resist? I can't.

'So you'd be a typical night-time ghost,' I say, glancing at Anna Gimblett to check she's listening. 'Wronged by the living, and returning in spirit form to right the wrong. You all know the difference between night ghosts and day ghosts, don't you?'

'I don't,' says Jenny Buckley.

No one knows. That's hardly surprising, since Lisa Paskin made it up and it's a load of rubbish. What's peculiar, though, is that Anna Gimblett is also shaking her head. She isn't saying, as I expected her to, 'Oh, I've heard this before from Lisa, Harriet's mum.'

I'm committed now; I have to explain. 'It's simple: the ghosts you see at night, they're the ghosts of good people who didn't deserve to die. They're back to get wrongs put right – wrongs that were done to them while they were alive. Daytime ghosts – the ones who stroll up to you in broad daylight and just start chatting like regular people – they weren't wronged. They were the bad guys. They're brazen, back to cause more trouble, and they'll use you to do it if they possibly can. That's why they're not scary when you see them. They have to present themselves as ordinary, non-threatening, even likeable human beings or else they won't be able to influence you, and that's what daylight ghosts are after: influence. They don't want to scare you or upset you – they want to be your friend.'

'You don't honestly believe that, do you?' Jenny Buckley asks.

Anna Gimblett snorts. 'It's the silliest thing I've ever heard,' she says.

'But you believe in ghosts, don't you, Anna?' I give her a sharp look. Surely she remembers hearing all this from Lisa. Why doesn't she mention it?

'Well, I believe in something beyond material reality, yes, but I certainly don't – '

'Anna, seriously?' Julie wrinkles her nose in distaste. 'You believe in ghosts?'

'According to Lisa, you've seen one yourself,' I chip in.

All the women turn to face me. There's silence for a few seconds. 'Lisa who?' asks Jenny.

'Lisa Paskin. Harriet's mum.'

They exchange puzzled looks. 'Who's Harriet?' Anna Gimblett asks.

'Oh, come on. Harriet's new in the same class as . . .' I stop. They're all staring.

'Mel, the newest girl in the class is your Bee,' says Anna. 'You must know that. No one's joined since last term.'

A gold envelope. A day off work. A hand in a drawer in an empty classroom at lunchtime. A little bitch that deserves everything she gets . . .

The images flash through my mind like cards shuffled too fast to see properly. The story so far . . .

What's going to happen in the end, Mel? Together we can make it happen.

I mustn't mention Lisa again. No one else knows about her. I don't want to alert them to the danger.

Grace Taggart can't be the only one who gets what she deserves. Of course she can't. What sort of justice is that?

———

AT HOME LATER that night, I turn on my computer and search the internet for the names Lisa and Harriet Paskin. I find many newspaper articles. In the accompanying photographs, I recognise my new friend from the school gates. Six years ago, Lisa and her daughter Harriet killed a teacher at eleven-year-old Harriet's school. They never revealed why they did it, though they did immediately confess to the crime, and there was never any doubt that they were guilty. Mother and daughter planned and committed the murder together. The teacher's husband shot them both dead on the steps of the crown court and is now in prison. This all happened in Cornwall, nowhere near our school.

Why did they do it? There appears to be no answer, at least not on the internet.

Feeling calmer than I have for a long time – almost completely removed from my actions – I search for 'ghosts who appear during the daytime' and variations on that theme. I find nothing, but I keep looking.

My hand in a gold envelope . . .

My phone buzzes on the table next to me. I pick it up. A new email has arrived from Jenny Buckley, the words 'Nice photo from tonight!' in the subject box. I click to open the photo and see us all sitting around the table: all the other mums in their ridiculous finery and me in my casual shirt with not-entirely-clean hair and no make-up.

Wait. What's Rachel Taggart doing there, in the picture? She wasn't there. She didn't come.

Her face is white, her eyes half closed. She's dead. I look at the other faces and see that they are all dead, in fact – all propped up at the table like stiff dolls.

Poison in the curry. A private room. Maybe someone's house, not a restaurant.

Julie, dead. Jenny, dead. Anna, dead. Rachel, dead. All the others, too. Not me; I'm not in this picture.

As soon as I've seen the whole story, it's gone. The photo on my phone's screen is, once again, the one Jenny sent me: all the mums smiling. *All the dead mothers of my daughter's friends.* I can't wait for our next Long-Overdue Mums' Night Out.

An Excerpt from
Closed Casket

1

A New Will

MICHAEL GATHERCOLE STARED at the closed door in front of him and tried to persuade himself that now was the moment to knock, as the aged grandfather clock in the hall downstairs stuttered its announcement of the hour.

Gathercole's instructions had been to present himself at four, and four it was. He had stood here – in this same spot on the wide first landing of Lillieoak – many times in the past six years. Only once had he felt less at ease than he did today. On that occasion he had been one of two men waiting, not alone as he was this afternoon. He still remembered every word of his conversation with the other man, when his preference would have been to recall none of it. Applying the self-discipline upon which he relied, he cast it from his mind.

He had been warned that he would find this afternoon's meeting difficult. The warning had formed part of the summons, which was typical of his hostess. "What I intend to say to you will come as a shock . . ."

Gathercole did not doubt it. The prior notice was no use to him, for it contained no information about what sort of preparation might be in order.

His discomfort grew more pronounced when he consulted his pocket watch and noticed that by hesitating, and with all the taking out of the watch and putting it back in the waistcoat pocket, and pulling it out once more to check, he had made himself late. It was already a minute after four o'clock. He knocked.

Only one minute late. She would notice – was there anything she did not notice? – but with any luck she would not remark upon it.

"Do come in, Michael!" Lady Athelinda Playford sounded as ebullient as ever. She was seventy years old, with a voice as strong and clear as a polished bell. Gathercole had never encountered her in sober spirits. There was always, with her, a cause for excitement – often such morsels as would alarm a conventional person. Lady Playford had a talent for extracting as much amusement from the inconsequential as from the controversial.

Gathercole had admired her stories of happy children solving mysteries that confounded the local police since he had first discovered them as a lonely ten-year-old in a London orphanage. Six years ago, he had met their creator for the first time and found her as disarming and unpredictable as her books. He had never expected to go far in his chosen profession, but here he was, thanks to Athelinda Playford: still a relatively young man at thirty-six, and a partner in a successful firm of solicitors, Gathercole and Rolfe. The notion that any profitable enterprise bore his name was still perplexing to Gathercole, even after a number of years.

His loyalty to Lady Playford surpassed all other attachments he had formed in his life, but personal acquaintance with his favorite author had forced him to admit to himself that he preferred shocks and startling about-turns to occur in the safely distant world of fiction, not in reality. Lady Playford, needless to say, did not share his preference.

He started to open the door.

"Are you going to . . . Ah! There you are! Don't hover. Sit, sit. We'll get nowhere if we don't start."

Gathercole sat.

"Hello, Michael." She smiled at him, and he had the strange sense he always had – as if her eyes had picked him up, turned him around and put him down again. "And now *you* must say, 'Hello, Athie.' Go on, say it! After all this time, it ought to be a breeze. Not 'Good afternoon, your ladyship.' Not 'Good day, Lady Playford.' A plain, friendly 'Hello, Athie.' Is that too much to manage? Ha!" She clapped her hands together. "You look quite the hunted fox cub! You can't understand why you've been invited to stay for a week, can you? Or why Mr. Rolfe was invited too."

Would the arrangements that Gathercole had put in place be sufficient to cover the absence of himself and

Orville Rolfe? It was unheard of for them both to be away from the office for five consecutive days, but Lady Playford was the firm's most illustrious client; no request from her could be refused.

"I daresay you are wondering if there will be other guests, Michael. We shall come to all of that, but I'm still waiting for you to say hello."

He had no choice. The greeting she demanded from him each time would never fall naturally from his lips. He was a man who liked to follow rules, and if there wasn't a rule forbidding a person of his background from addressing a dowager viscountess, widow of the fifth Viscount Playford of Clonakilty, as "Athie," then Gathercole fervently believed there ought to be.

It was unfortunate, therefore – he said so to himself often – that Lady Playford, for whom he would do anything, poured scorn on the rules at every turn and derided those who obeyed them as "dreary dry sticks."

"Hello, Athie."

"There we are!" She spread out her arms in the manner of a woman inviting a man to leap into them, though Gathercole knew that was not her intention. "Ordeal survived. You may relax. Not too much! We have important matters to attend to – after we've discussed the bundle of the moment."

It was Lady Playford's habit to describe the book she was in the middle of writing as "the bundle." Her latest sat on the corner of the desk and she threw a resentful glance in its direction. It looked to Gathercole less like a novel in progress and more like a whirlwind represented

in paper: creased pages with curled edges, corners pointing every which way. There was nothing in the least rect-
angular about it.

Lady Playford hauled herself out of her armchair
by the window. She never looked out, Gathercole had
noticed. If there was a human being to inspect, Lady
Playford did not waste time on nature. Her study offered
the most magnificent views: the rose garden, and, behind
it, a perfectly square lawn, at the center of which was the
angel statue that her husband, Guy, the late Viscount
Playford, had commissioned as a wedding anniversary
gift, to celebrate thirty years of marriage.

Gathercole always looked at the statue and the lawn
and the rosebushes when he visited, as well as at the
grandfather clock in the hall and the bronze table lamp
in the library with the leaded glass snail-shell shade;
he made a point of doing so. He approved of the stabil-
ity they seemed to offer. Things – by which Gathercole
meant lifeless objects and not any more general state of
affairs – rarely changed at Lillieoak. Lady Playford's constant meticulous scrutiny of every person who crossed
her path meant that she paid little attention to anything
that could not speak.

In her study, the room she and Gathercole were in
now, there were two books upside down in the large
bookcase that stood against one wall: *Shrimp Seddon and
the Pearl Necklace* and *Shrimp Seddon and the Christmas
Stocking*. They had been upside down since Gathercole's
first visit. Six years later, to see them righted would be
disconcerting. No other author's books were permitted

to reside upon those shelves, only Athelinda Playford's. Their spines brought some much-needed brightness into the wood-paneled room – strips of red, blue, green, purple, orange; colors designed to appeal to children – though even they were no match for Lady Playford's lustrous cloud of silver hair.

She positioned herself directly in front of Gathercole. "I want to talk to you about my will, Michael, and to ask a favor of you. But first: how much do you imagine a child – an ordinary child – might know about surgical procedures to reshape a nose?"

"A . . . a nose?" Gathercole wished he could hear about the will first and the favor second. Both sounded important, and were perhaps related. Lady Playford's testamentary arrangements had been in place for some time. All was as it should be. Could it be that she wanted to change something?

"Don't be exasperating, Michael. It's a perfectly simple question. After a bad motorcar accident, or to correct a deformity. Surgery to change the shape of the nose. Would a child know about such a thing? Would he know its name?"

"I don't know, I'm afraid."

"Do *you* know its name?"

"Surgery, I should call it, whether it's for the nose or any other part of the body."

"I suppose you might know the name without knowing you know it. That happens sometimes." Lady Playford frowned. "Hmph. Let me ask you another question: you arrive at the offices of a firm that employs ten men and two women. You overhear a few of the men talking about one of the women. They refer to her as 'Rhino.'"

"Hardly gallant of them."

"Their manners are not your concern. A few moments later, the two ladies return from lunch. One of them is fine-boned, slender and mild in her temperament, but she has a rather peculiar face. No one knows what's wrong with it, but it somehow doesn't look quite right. The other is a mountain of a woman – twice my size at least." Lady Playford was of average height, and plump, with downward slopes for shoulders that gave her a rather funnel-like appearance. "What is more, she has a fierce look on her face. Now, which of the two women I've described would you guess to be Rhino?"

"The large, fierce one," Gathercole replied at once.

"Excellent! You're wrong. In my story, Rhino turns out to be the slim girl with the strange facial features – because, you see, she's had her nose surgically reconstructed after an accident, in a procedure that goes by the name of *rhino*plasty!"

"Ah. That I did not know," said Gathercole.

"But I fear children won't know the name, and that's who I'm writing for. If *you* haven't heard of rhinoplasty . . ." Lady Playford sighed. "I'm in two minds. I was so excited when I first thought of it, but then I started to worry. Is it a little too scientific to have the crux of the story revolving around a medical procedure? No one really thinks about surgeries unless they have to, after all – unless they're about to go into hospital themselves. Children don't think about such things, do they?"

"I like the idea," said Gathercole. "You might emphasize that the slender lady has not merely a strange face but a strange *nose*, to send your readers in the right direction. You could say early on in the story that she has a new nose, thanks to expert surgery, and you could have Shrimp somehow find out the name of the operation and let the reader see her surprise when she finds out."

Shrimp Seddon was Lady Playford's ten-year-old fictional heroine, the leader of a gang of child detectives.

"So the reader sees the surprise but not, at first, the discovery. Yes! And perhaps Shrimp could say to Podge, 'You'll never guess what it's called,' and then be interrupted, and I can put in a chapter there about something else – maybe the police stupidly arresting the wrong person but even wronger than usual, maybe even Shrimp's father or mother – so that anyone reading can go away and consult a doctor or an encyclopedia if they wish. But I won't leave it *too* long before Shrimp reveals all. *Yes*. Michael, I knew I could rely on you. That's settled, then. Now, about my will . . ."

She returned to her chair by the window and arranged herself in it. "I want you to make a new one for me."

Gathercole was surprised. According to the terms of Lady Playford's existing will, her substantial estate was to be divided equally, upon her death, between her two surviving children: her daughter, Claudia, and her son, Harry, the sixth Viscount Playford of Clonakilty. There had been a third child, Nicholas, but he had died young.

"I want to leave everything to my secretary, Joseph Scotcher," announced the clear-as-a-bell voice.

Gathercole sat forward in his chair. It was pointless to try to push the unwelcome words away. He had heard them, and could not pretend otherwise.

What act of vandalism was Lady Playford about to insist upon? She could not be in earnest. This was a trick; it had to be. Yes, Gathercole saw what she was about: get the frivolous part out of the way first – Rhino, rhino-plasty, all very clever and amusing – and then introduce the big caper as if it were a serious proposition.

"I am in my right mind and entirely serious, Michael. I'd like you to do as I ask. Before dinner tonight, please. Why don't you make a start now?"

"Lady Playford . . ."

"Athie," she corrected him.

"If this is something else from your Rhino story that you're trying out on me – "

"Sincerely, it is not, Michael. I have never lied to you. I am not lying now. I need you to draw me up a new will. Joseph Scotcher is to inherit everything."

"But what about your children?"

"Claudia is about to marry a greater fortune than mine, in the shape of Randall Kimpton. She will be perfectly all right. And Harry has a good head on his shoulders and a dependable if enervating wife. Poor Joseph needs what I have to give more than Claudia or Harry."

"I must appeal to you to think very carefully before – "

"Michael, please don't make a cake of yourself." Lady Playford cut him off. "Do you imagine the idea first occurred to me as you knocked at the door a few minutes ago? Or is it more likely that I have been ruminating on this for weeks or months? The careful thought you urge upon me has taken place, I assure you. Now: are you going to witness my new will or must I call for Mr. Rolfe?"

So that was why Orville Rolfe had also been invited to Lillieoak: in case he, Gathercole, refused to do her bidding.

"There's another change I'd like to make to my will at the same time: the favor I mentioned, if you recall. To this part, you may say no if you wish, but I do hope you won't. At present, Claudia and Harry are named as my literary executors. That arrangement no longer suits me. I should be honored if *you*, Michael, would agree to take on the role."

"To . . . to be your literary executor?" He could scarcely credit it. For nearly a minute, he felt too overwhelmed to speak. Oh, but it was all *wrong*. What would Lady Playford's children have to say about it? He couldn't accept.

"Do Harry and Claudia know your intentions?" he asked eventually.

"No. They will at dinner tonight. Joseph too. At present the only people who know are you and me."

"Has there been a conflict within the family of which I am unaware?"

"Not at all!" Lady Playford smiled. "Harry, Claudia and I are the best of friends – until dinner tonight, at least."

"I . . . but . . . you have known Joseph Scotcher a mere six years. You met him the day you met me."

"There is no need to tell me what I already know, Michael."

"Whereas your children . . . Additionally, my under-standing was that Joseph Scotcher . . ."

"*Speak*, dear man."

"Is Scotcher not seriously ill?" Silently, Gathercole added: *Do you no longer believe he will die before you?*

Athelinda Playford was not young but she was full of vitality. It was hard to believe that anyone who relished life as she did might be deprived of it.

"Indeed, Joseph is very sick," she said. "He grows weaker by the day. Hence this unusual decision on my part. I have never said so before, but I trust you're aware that I adore Joseph? I love him like a son – as if he were my own flesh and blood."

Gathercole felt a sudden tightness in his chest. Yes, he'd been aware. The difference between knowing a thing and having it confirmed was vast. It led to thoughts that were beneath him, which he fought to banish.

"Joseph tells me his doctors have said he has only weeks, now, to live."

"But . . . then I'm afraid I'm quite baffled," said Gathercole. "You wish to make a new will in favor of a man you know won't be around to make use of his inheritance."

"Nothing is ever known for certain in this world, Michael."

"And if Scotcher should succumb to his illness within weeks, as you expect him to – what then?"

"Why, in that eventuality we revert to the original plan – Harry and Claudia get half each."

"I must ask you something," said Gathercole, in whom a painful anxiety had started to grow. "Forgive the impertinence. Do you have any reason to believe that you too will die imminently?"

"Me?" Lady Playford laughed. "I'm strong as an ox. I expect to chug on for years."

"Then Scotcher will inherit nothing on your demise, being long dead himself, and the new will you are asking me to arrange will achieve nothing but to create discord between you and your children."

"On the contrary: my new will might cause *something wonderful* to happen." She said this with relish.

Gathercole sighed. "I'm afraid to say I'm still baffled."

"Of course you are," said Athelinda Playford. "I knew you would be."

An Excerpt from
A Game for All the Family

THE PEOPLE I'M about to meet in my new life, if they're anything like the ones I'm leaving behind, will ask as soon as they can get away with it. In my fantasy, they don't have faces or names, only voices – raised, but not excessively so; determinedly casual.

What do you do?

Does anyone still add "for a living" to the end of that question? It sounds stupidly old-fashioned.

I hope they miss out the "living" bit, because this has nothing to do with how I plan to fund my smoked-salmon-for-breakfast habit. I want my faceless new acquaintances to care only about how I spend my time and define myself – what I believe to be the point of me. That's why I need the question to arrive in its purest form.

I have the perfect answer: one word long, with plenty of space around it.

Nothing.

Everything should be surrounded by as much space as possible: people, houses, words. That's part of the reason for starting a new life. In my old one, there wasn't enough space of any kind.

My name is Justine Merrison and I do Nothing. With a capital N. Not a single thing. I'll have to try not to throw back my head and laugh after saying it, or sprint a victory lap around whoever was unfortunate enough to ask me. Ideally, the question will come from people who do Something: surveyors, lawyers, supermarket managers – all haggard and harried from a six-month stretch of fourteen-hour working days.

I won't mention what I used to do, or talk about day-to-day chores as if they count as Something. Yes, it's true that I'll have to do some boiling of pasta in my new life, and some throwing of socks into washing machines, but that will be as easy and automatic as breathing. I don't intend to let trivial day-to-day stuff get in the way of my central project, which is to achieve a state of all-embracing inactivity.

"Nothing," I will say boldly and proudly, in the way that another person might say "Neuroradiology." Then I'll smile, as glowing white silence slides in to hug the curved edges of the word. *Nothing.*

"What are you grinning about?" Alex asks. Unlike me, he isn't imagining a calm, soundless state. He is firmly embedded in our real-world surroundings: six lanes of futile horn-beep gripes and suffocating exhaust fumes. "The joys of the A406," he muttered half an hour ago, as we added ourselves to the long line of backed-up traffic.

For me, the congestion is a joy. It reminds me that I don't need to do anything in a hurry. At this rate of travel – approximately four meters per hour, which is unusual even for the North Circular – we won't get to Devon before midnight. *Excellent.* Let it take twenty hours, or thirty. Our new house will still be there tomorrow, and the day after. It doesn't matter when I arrive, as I have nothing pressing to attend to. I won't need to down a quick cup of tea, then immediately start hectoring a telecommunications company about how soon they can hook me up with WiFi. I have no urgent emails to send.

"Hello? Justine?" Alex calls out, in case I didn't hear his question over the noise of Georges Bizet's *Carmen* that's blaring from our car's speakers. A few minutes ago, he and Ellen were singing along, having adapted the words somewhat: "Stuck, stuck in traffic, traffic, stuck, stuck in traffic, traffic, stuck, stuck in traffic, traffic *jam*. Stuck, stuck in traffic, traffic, stuck, stuck in traffic, traffic *jam*, traffic *jam*, traffic *jam* . . ."

"Mum!" Ellen yells behind me. "Dad's talking to you!"

"I think your mother's in a trance, El. Must be the heat."

It would never occur to Alex to turn off music in order to speak. For him, silence is there to be packed as full as possible, like an empty bag. The Something that he does – has for as long as I've known him – is singing. Opera. He travels all over the world, is away for one week in every three, on average, and loves every second of his home-is-where-the-premiere-is existence. Which is lucky. If I didn't know he was idyllically happy with his hectic, spotlit life, I might not be able to enjoy my Nothing to the full. I might feel guilty.

As it is, we'll be able to share our contrasting triumphs without either of us resenting the other. Alex will tell me that he managed to squeeze four important calls into the time between the airline staff telling him to switch off his phone, and them noticing that he'd disobeyed them and telling him again like they really meant it this time. I'll tell him about reading in the bath for hours, topping up with hot water again and again, almost too lazy to twist the tap.

I press the "off" button on the CD player, unwilling to compete with *Carmen*, and tell Alex about my little question-and-answer fantasy. He laughs. Ellen says, "You're a nutter, Mum. You can't say 'Nothing.' You'll scare people."

"Good. They can fear me first, then they can envy me, and wonder if they might take up doing Nothing themselves. Think how many lives I could save."

"No, they'll think you're a depressed housewife who's going to go home and swallow a bottle of pills."

"Abandoned and neglected by her jet-setting husband," Alex adds, wiping sweat from his brow with the sleeve of his shirt.

"No they won't," I say. "Not if I beam blissfully while describing my completely empty schedule."

"Ah, so you *will* say more than 'Nothing'!"

"Say you're a stay-at-home mum," Ellen advises. "Or you're taking a career break after a stressful few years. You're weighing up various options . . ."

"But I'm not. I've already chosen Nothing. Hey." I tap Alex on the arm. "I'm going to buy one of those year-planner wall charts – a really beautiful one – and stick it up in a prominent place, so that I can leave every day's box totally empty. Three hundred and sixty-five empty boxes. It'll be a thing of beauty."

"You're *so annoying*, Mum," Ellen groans. "You keep banging on about this new life and how everything's going to be so different, but it won't be, because . . . you! You're incapable of changing. You're *exactly the same*: still a massive . . . zealot. You were a zealot about working, and now you're going to be one about not working. It'll be so boring for me. And embarrassing."

"Pipe down, pipsqueak," I say in a tone of mock outrage. "Aren't you, like, supposed to be, like, only thirteen?"

"I haven't said 'like' for ages, actually, apart from to express approval," Ellen protests.

"That's true, she hasn't," says Alex. "And she's frighteningly spot-on about her drama-queen mother. Tell me this: if you crave tranquility as you claim to, why are you daydreaming about starting fights with strangers?"

"Good point!" Ellen crows.

"Fights? What fights?"

"Don't feign innocence."

"Not feigning!" I say indignantly.

Alex rolls his eyes. "Aggressively saying, 'Nothing' when people ask you what you do, making them feel uncomfortable by refusing to qualify it at all, or explain . . ."

"Not aggressively. *Happily* saying it. And there's nothing about Nothing to explain."

"Smugly," Alex says. "Which is a form of aggression. Flaunting your pleasurable idleness in the faces of those with oversensitive work ethics and overstuffed diaries. It's sadistic."

"You might have a point," I concede. "I've been particularly looking forward to telling the hardworking, stressed people I meet that I do Nothing. The more relaxed a person looks, the less fun it'll be to boast to them. And it's pointless bragging to the likes of you – you love your overstuffed diary. So I'm just going to have to hope I meet lots of people who hate their demanding jobs but can't escape them. Oh God." I close my eyes. "It's sickeningly obvious, isn't it? It's me I want to taunt. My former self. That's who I'm angry with."

I could have escaped at any time. Could have walked away years earlier, instead of letting work swallow up my whole life.

"I literally cannot believe I have a mother who . . . homilies on in the way you do, Mum," Ellen grumbles. "None of my friends' mothers do it. *None*. They all say normal things, like 'No TV until you've done your homework' and 'Would you like some more lasagna?'"

"Yes, well, your mother can't go ten minutes without having a major, life-changing realization – can you, darling?"

"Fuck off! Oops." I giggle. If I've ever been happier than I am now, I can't remember the occasion.

"Aha! We're on the move again." Alex starts to sing, "End of the traffic, traffic, end of the traffic, traffic, end of the traffic, traffic *jam*, end of the traffic, traffic, end of the traffic, traffic *jam*, traffic *jam*, traffic *jam* . . ."

Poor, long-dead Georges Bizet. I'm sure this wasn't the legacy he had in mind.

"Excuse me while I don't celebrate," says Ellen. "We've still got another, what, seven hours before we get there? I'm boiling. When are we going to get a car with air-conditioning that works?"

"I don't believe any car air-conditioning works," I tell her. "It's like windshield wipers. The other cars want you to think they've got it figured out, but they're all hot and stuffy on days like today, whatever Jeremy Clarkson might want us to think. They all have wipers that squeak like bats being garroted."

"Aaand . . . we're at a standstill again," says Alex, shaking his head. "The golden age of being in transit was short-lived. You're wrong about the seven hours, though, El. Quite, quite wrong."

"Yeah, it's just doubled to fourteen," Ellen says bitterly.

"Wrong. Mum and I didn't say anything because we wanted to surprise you, but actually . . . we're very nearly there."

I smile at Ellen in the rearview mirror. She's hiding behind her thick, dark brown hair, trying to hang on to her disgruntled mood and not succumb to laughter. Alex is a rotten practical joker. His ideas are imaginative enough, but he's scuppered every time by his special prankster voice, instantly recognizable to anyone who has known him longer than a week.

"Yeah right, Dad. We're still on the North Circular and we're very nearly in Devon. Of course." Big, beautiful green eyes and heavy sarcasm: two things I adore about my daughter.

"No, not Devon. There's been a change of plan. We didn't want to inconvenience you with a long drive, so . . . we've sold Speedwell House and bought that one instead!" Alex points out of the car window to a squat redbrick 1930s-or-thereabouts semi-detached house. I know immediately which one he means. It looks ridiculous. It's the one anyone would single out, the last in a row of eight. There are three signs attached to its façade, all too big for such a small building.

My skin feels hot and tingly all of a sudden. Like when I had cellulitis on my leg after getting bitten by a mosquito in Corfu, except this time it's my whole body.

I stare at the house with the signs. Silently, I instruct the traffic not to move so that I can examine it for as long as I need to.

Why do I need to?

Apart from the excessive ornamentation, there is nothing to distinguish this house from any other 1930s redbrick semi. One sign, the largest – in the top right-hand corner, above a bedroom window – says "Panama Row." That must refer to all the houses huddled bravely together, facing six lanes of roaring traffic immediately outside their windows.

The other two signs – one missing a screw and leaning down on one side and the other visibly grime-streaked – are the name and number of the house. I try to make myself look away, but I can't. I read both and have opinions about them, positive and negative.

That's right: number 8. Yes, it's called . . . No. No, that isn't its name.

Pressure is building in my eyes, head, chest. Thrumming.

I wait until the worst of it subsides, then look down at my arms. They look ordinary. No goosebumps. *Impossible. I can feel them: prickly lumps under my skin.*

"Our new house appears to be called 'German,'" says Alex. "Ludicrous name! I mean, er, won't it be fun to live in a house called 'German,' El?"

"No, because we're not going to be living there. As if Mum'd agree to buy a house on a nearly motorway!"

"You know why she agreed? Because, in no more than ten minutes, we'll take a left turn, then another left, and we'll have arrived. No more long journey, just home sweet home. As the old Chinese proverb says, 'He who buys a beautiful house in the countryside far away might never get there, and may as well buy an ugly house on the North Circular and have done with it.'"

"It's not ugly," I manage to say, though my throat is so tight, I can hardly speak.

It's lovely. It's safe. Stop the car.

I'm not looking at number 8 Panama Row anymore. I tore my eyes away, and now I must make sure they stay away. That won't be hard. I'm too scared to look again.

"Mum? What's wrong? You sound weird."

"You look weird," says Alex. "Justine? Are you okay? You're shivering."

"No," I whisper. "I'm not." *Not okay. Yes, shivering. Too hot, but shivering.* I want to clarify, but my tongue is paralyzed.

"What's wrong?"

"I . . ."

"Mum, you're scaring me. What is it?"

"It's not called 'German.' Some of the letters have fallen off." How do I know this? I've never seen 8 Panama Row before in my life. Never heard of it, known about it, been anywhere near it.

"Oh yeah," says Ellen. "She's right, Dad. You can see where the other letters were."

"But I didn't see it. I . . . I *knew* the name wasn't German. It had nothing to do with what I saw."

"Justine, calm down. Nothing to do with what you saw? That makes no sense."

"It's obvious there are letters missing," says Ellen. "There's loads of empty sign left at the end of the name. Who would call a house 'German,' anyway?"

What should I do and say? I'd tell Alex the truth if we were alone.

"Dad? Accelerate? Like, you're holding everyone up. Ugh! I said 'like' again, goddammit."

"Don't say 'goddammit' either," Alex tells her.

"Don't let me watch *The Good Wife*, then. And you two swear *all the time*, hypocrites."

The car creeps forward, then picks up speed. I feel braver as soon as I know it's no longer possible for me to see 8 Panama Row. "That was . . . strange," I say. *The strangest thing that has ever happened to me.* I exhale slowly.

"What, Mum?"

"Yes, tell us, goddammit."

"Dad! Objection! Sustained."

"Overruled, actually. You can't sustain your own objection. Anyway, shush, will you?"

Shush. Shut up, shut up, shut up. It's not funny. Nothing about this is funny.

"Justine, what's the matter with you?" Alex is more patient than I am. I'd be raising my voice by now.

"That house. You pointed, and I looked, and I had this . . . this overwhelmingly strong feeling of *yes*. Yes, that's my house. I wanted to fling open the car door and run to it."

"Except you don't live there, so that's mad. You don't live anywhere at the moment. Until this morning you lived in London, and hopefully by this evening you'll live just outside Kingswear in Devon, but you currently live nowhere."

How appropriate. Do Nothing, live nowhere.

"You certainly don't live in an interwar semi beside the A406, so you can relax." Alex's tone is teasing but not unkind. I'm relieved that he doesn't sound worried. He sounds less concerned now than he did before; the direction of travel reassures me.

"I know I don't live there. I can't explain it. I had a powerful feeling that I belonged in that house. Or belonged *to* it, somehow. By 'powerful,' I mean like a physical assault."

"Lordy McSwordy," Ellen mumbles from the back seat.

"Almost a premonition that I'll live there one day." How can I phrase it to make it sound more rational? "I'm not saying it's true. Now that the feeling's passed, I can hear how daft it sounds, but when I first looked, when you pointed at it, there was no doubt in my mind."

"Justine, nothing in the world could ever induce you to live cheek by jowl with six lanes of traffic," says Alex. "You haven't changed *that* much. Is this a joke?"

"No."

"I know what it is: poverty paranoia. You're worried about you not earning, us taking on a bigger mortgage . . . Have you had nightmares about losing your teeth?"

"My teeth?"

"I read somewhere that teeth-loss dreams mean anxiety about money."

"It isn't that."

"Even poor, you wouldn't live in that house – not unless you were kidnapped and held prisoner there."

"Dad," says Ellen. "Is it time for your daily You're-Not-Helping reminder?"

Alex ignores her. "Have you got something to drink?" he asks me. "You're probably dehydrated. Heatstroke."

"Yes." There's water in my bag, by my feet.

"Drink it, then."

I don't want to. Not yet. As soon as I pull out the bottle and open it, this conversation will be over; Alex will change the subject to something less inexplicable. I can't talk about anything else until I understand what's just happened to me.

"Oh no. Look: roadwork." When Alex starts to sing again, I don't know what's happening at first, even though it's the same tune from *Carmen* and only the words have changed. Ellen joins in. Soon they're singing in unison, "Hard hats and yellow jackets, hard hats and yellow jackets, hard hats and yellow jackets, *boo*. Hard hats and yellow jackets, hard hats and yellow jackets, boo, sod it, boo, sod it, *boo* . . ."

Or I could try to forget about it. With every second that passes, that seems more feasible. I feel almost as I did before Alex pointed at the house. I could maybe convince myself that I imagined the whole thing.

Go on, then. Tell yourself that.

The voice in my head is not quite ready. It's still repeating words from the script I've instructed it to discard:

One day, 8 Panama Row – a house you would not choose in a million years – will be your home, and you won't mind the traffic at all. You'll be so happy and grateful to live there, you won't be able to believe your luck.

FOUR MONTHS LATER

Family Tree
The Ingreys of Speedwell House

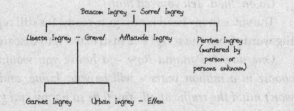

Bascom Ingrey — Sorrel Ingrey

Lisette Ingrey — Grevel   Allsande Ingrey   Perrine Ingrey
(murdered by
person or
persons unknown)

Garnet Ingrey   Urban Ingrey — Ellen

Murder Mystery Story

by Ellen Colley, Class 9G
Chapter 1

~

The Killing of Malachy Dodd

PERRINE INGREY DROPPED Malachy Dodd out of a window. She wanted to kill him and she succeeded. Later, no one believed her when she screamed, "I didn't do it!"

Both of their families, the Ingreys and the Dodds, knew that Perrine and Malachy had been upstairs in a room together with no one else around.

This was Perrine's bedroom. It had a tiny wooden door (painted mint green, Perrine's favorite color) next to her bed. This little door was the only way of getting from one part of the upstairs of Speedwell House to the other unless you wanted to go back downstairs, through the living room and the library, and then climb up a different lot of stairs, and no one ever wanted to do that. They preferred to bend themselves into a quarter of the size of the shortest dwarf in the world (because that was how tiny the mint-green door was) and squeeze themselves through the minuscule space.

After she dropped Malachy out of the window and watched him fall to his gory death on the terrace below, Perrine squashed herself through the tiny green door and pulled it shut behind her. When her parents found her huddled on the landing on the other side, she exclaimed, "But I wasn't even in the room when it happened!"

Nobody was convinced. Perrine hadn't been clever enough to move a decent distance away from the door, so it was obvious she had just come through it. Her second mistake was to yell, "He fell out by accident!" For one thing Malachy was not tall enough to fall out of the window accidentally (all the adults agreed later that his center of gravity was too low) and for another, if Perrine wasn't in the room when it happened, how did she know that he fell by accident?

A third big *clue* was that every single other person who might have murdered Malachy was downstairs in the dining room at the time of his hideous death. All of the Dodds were there, and all the Ingreys apart from Perrine. Her two older sisters, Lisette and Allisande, were sitting in chairs facing the three sets of French doors that were open onto the terrace where Malachy fell, splattering his red and gray blood and brains on the ground beside the fountain. It felt as if his falling shook the whole house, especially the French "purple crystals" chandelier above Lisette and Allisande's heads, but that must have been an illusion.

Lisette and Allisande definitely saw Malachy fall and smash, however, and, what's more, they heard a loud, triumphant "Ha!" floating down from above. Both of them recognized the voice of their younger sister, Perrine.

So, if all the other possible suspects were in the dining room, who else apart from Perrine Ingrey could have been responsible for Malachy landing in a heap on the paving slabs? I'll tell you who: nobody.

There was no doubt that Perrine killed him, however much she wailed that she was innocent. (The death of Malachy Dodd is not the murder mystery in this story. The mystery is who murdered Perrine Ingrey, because she went on to get murdered too, but that comes later.)

No, there was nothing mysterious about the cruel killing of Malachy. Both of the families, the Ingreys and the Dodds, knew the truth, and soon everybody in Kingswear and the surrounding towns and villages knew it too. You cannot keep anything quiet in a place like Devon, where the main hobby is spreading cream and jam onto scones and gossiping about everything you've heard that day.

It came as a surprise to absolutely nobody that one of the Ingreys had committed a murder, because they were such a weird family – the weirdest that Kingswear and its environs had ever known. But there was one big shock for everyone when they heard the news. People should have realized that the most bizarre family for miles around would do the opposite of what you'd expect, or else they would have no right to retain their title of weirdest family. And what most of the nearby town and village folk would have expected was that if 1) there was a murder and 2) the killer was one of the three Ingrey sisters, it was bound to be either Lisette, the eldest, or Allisande, the middle sister. Certainly not Perrine, the youngest, who was the only one who had had what you might call a properly balanced upbringing.

You see, unlike most parents, especially so long ago, Bascom and Sorrel Ingrey couldn't

1

ELLEN?" I KNOCK on her bedroom door, even though it's ajar and I can see her sitting on her bed. When she doesn't respond, I walk in. "What's this?" I hold up the papers.

She doesn't look at me, but continues to stare out of the window. I can't help looking too. I still haven't gotten used to the beauty of where we live. Ellen's room and the kitchen directly beneath it have the best views in the house: the fountain and gazebo to the left, and, straight ahead, the gentle downward curve of the grass bank that stretches all the way from our front door to the River Dart, studded with rhododendrons, magnolia trees, camellias. When we first came to see Speedwell House in April, there were bluebells, primroses, cyclamen and periwinkles in bloom, poking out of ground ivy and grass: little bursts of brightness interrupting the lush green. I can't wait for those spots of color to reappear next spring.

In the distance, the water sparkles in the bright light like a flowing liquid diamond. On the other side of the river, there's wooded hillside with a few wooden boat-houses down at the bottom, and, above them, a scatter-ing of pink, yellow and white cottages protruding from the greenery. From this distance, it looks as if someone has dropped pick-and-mix sweets from the window of an airplane and they've landed among the trees.

Since we moved here, Alex has said at least three times, "It's a funny thing about the English coastline: the land just stops. It's like the interior of the country, and then it suddenly plunges into the sea without any interim bit. I mean, look." At this point he always nods across the river. "That could be in the middle of the Peak District."

I don't know what he means. Maybe I'm shallow, but I don't much care about understanding the scenery. If it looks gorgeous, that's good enough for me.

Boats drift past: sailing dinghies, small yachts, plea-sure boats and the occasional schooner. There's one pass-ing now that looks like a child's sketch of a boat: wooden, with a mast and a red sail. Most have less elegant outlines and would be fiddlier to draw.

These are the things I can see out of Ellen's window. Can she see any of them? She's looking out, but there's a shut-off air about her, as if she's not really present in the room with me.

"El. What's this?" I say again, waving the pieces of paper at her. I don't like what I've read. I don't like it at all, however imaginative and accomplished a piece of writing it might be for a fourteen-year-old. It scares me.

"What's what?" Ellen says tonelessly.

"This family tree and beginning of a story about a family called the Ingreys."

"It's for school."

Worst possible answer. Too short, too lacking in attitude. The Ellen I know – the Ellen I desperately miss – would have said, "Um, it's a family tree? And a story about a family called the Ingreys? The answer's kind of contained in the question." How long has it been since she last yelled "Objection!" swiftly followed by "Sustained!"? At least a month.

Whatever Alex says, there's something wrong with our daughter. He doesn't see it because he doesn't want it to be true. When he's home, she makes a special effort to be normal in front of him. She knows that if she can fool him, he'll do his best to persuade me that I'm wrong, that this is standard teenage behavior.

I know it's not true. I know my daughter, and this isn't her. This isn't how even the most alarming teenage version of her would behave.

Bascom and Sorrel Ingrey. It's Ellen's handwriting, but I don't believe she would have made up those names. Allisande, Malachy Dodd, Garnet and Urban . . . Could she have copied it out from somewhere?

I'm trying to work out how I can tactfully ask what prompted her to invent the alarming Perrine Ingrey, whom I resent for splattering my lovely terrace with blood and brains and celebrating with a "Ha!," when the phone starts to ring downstairs. I would leave it, but it might be Alex. As I run to get it, I remind myself that I must call about having some more telephone points put in.

Must. I hate that word. In my old life, it meant "Move fast! Panic! Prepare for catastrophe! Turn it into success by the end of the day! Keep two people happy who want incompatible outcomes! Be brilliant or lose everything!" Fifty times a day, "must" could have signified any of those things, or all of them simultaneously.

I stop at the bottom of the stairs, out of breath. I refuse to hurry. *There is no urgency about anything. Calm down. Remember your mission and purpose. If you're fretting, you're not doing Nothing.*

I'm not going to worry about missing Alex's call. And if it isn't him on the phone, I'm not going to wonder why he hasn't called today. I know he's fine – being fawned over by acolytes in Berlin. Discussing the Ellen situation with him can wait.

Worries are pack animals as well as cowards: too flimsy and insubstantial to do much damage alone, they signal for backup. Pretty soon there's a whole gang of them circling you and you can't push your way out. *Stuff the lot of them,* I think as I cross the wide black and white tiled hall on my way to the kitchen. I'm lucky to be happy and to have this amazing new life. I don't have much to be anxious about, certainly not compared to most people. There are only two points of concern in my current existence: Ellen's odd behavior, and – though I'm ashamed to be obsessing about it still – the house by the side of the North Circular. 8 Panama Row.

I've dreamed about it often since the day we moved, dreamed of trying to get there – on foot, by car, by train – but never quite making it. The closest I got was in a taxi. The driver pulled up, and I climbed out and stood on the pavement. The front door of the house opened, and then I woke up.

I pick up the phone and say, "Hello?," remembering Alex's pretending-to-be-serious insistence that we must all from now on greet anyone who calls with the words "Speedwell House, good morning/afternoon/evening." "That's how people who live in big country piles answer their phones," he said. "I saw it on ... something, I'm sure."

Our new house's solitary phone is not portable. It's next to the kitchen window, attached to the wall by a curly wire that makes a plasticky squeaking sound when pulled. Finally at the age of forty-three I have a big, comfy sofa in a kitchen that isn't too small, and I'm unable to reach it to sit down when I make or answer a phone call. I have to stand and look at it instead, while imagining my legs are aching more than they are. My mobile can't help me; there's no reception inside the house yet. Coverage seems only to start at the end of our drive.

"Hello," I say again.

"It's me."

Not Alex. A woman whose voice I don't recognize. Someone arrogant enough to think that she and I are on "It's me" terms when we aren't. It should be easy enough to work out who, once she's said a few more words. I know lots of arrogant women, or at least I did in London. Arrogant men, too. I hoped never to hear from any of them again.

"Sorry, it's a terrible line," I lie. "I can hardly hear you." How embarrassing. *Come on, brain, tell me who this is before I'm forced to reveal how little this person matters to me.* Alex's mum? No. My stepmother? Definitely not.

"It's me. I can hear you perfectly."

A woman, for sure. With a voice as hard as granite and a slight . . . not quite lisp, but something similar. As if her tongue is impeded by her teeth, or she's speaking while trying to stop a piece of chewing gum from falling out of her mouth. Is she disguising her voice? Why would she do that if she wants me to recognize her?

"I'm sorry, this line is appalling. I honestly have no idea who I'm speaking to," I say.

Silence. Then a sigh, and a weary "I think we're beyond lying by now, aren't we? I know you came here to scare me, but it won't work."

I hold the phone away from my ear and stare at it. This is absurd. I've never heard this woman's voice before. She is nobody I know.

"This is a misunderstanding. I don't know who you think you're speaking to – "

"Oh, I know *exactly* who I'm speaking to."

"Well . . . lucky you. I wish I did. I don't recognize your voice. If I know you, you're going to have to remind me. And I've no idea what you mean, but I promise you, I didn't come here to scare you or anyone else."

"I've been frightened of you for too long. I'm not running away again."

I lean my forehead against the kitchen wall. "Look, shall we sort this out? It shouldn't take long. Who are you, and who do you think I am? Because whoever you think I am, I'm not. You're going to have to give your speech again to someone else." I should have hung up on her by now, but I'm holding out for a logical resolution. I want to hear her say, "Oh my God, I'm so sorry. I thought you were my abusive ex-boyfriend / delinquent child / tyrannical religious cult leader."

"I know who you are," says my anonymous caller. "And you know who I am."

"No, you evidently don't, and no I don't. My name is Justine Merrison. You're delivering your message to the wrong person."

"I'm not going to be intimidated by you," she says.

Should have hung up. Still should. "Good. Excellent," I say briskly. "Any chance that I could not be intimidated by you either? Like, no more crank calls? Is your No Intimidation policy one-way, or could it be reciprocal?"

I'm making jokes. How bizarre. If someone had asked me before today how I'd feel if an unpleasant-sounding stranger called and threatened me, I would probably have said I'd be frightened, but I'm not. This is too stupid. I'm too preoccupied by other, more important things, and even some unbelievably trivial ones, like the list pinned to the cork board on the wall opposite: tasks Alex has assigned to me. *Musts.* Call a landscape gardener, find a window cleaner, get the car valeted. Alex is trying to insist I use a local firm he found called The Car Men, because of the Bizet connection. He's written "CAR MEN!!" in capitals at the top of the list. The exclamation marks are intended to remind me that our Range Rover is a biohazard on wheels.

No, I'm sorry. Never make me look at a list again. Haven't you heard? I do Nothing.

Apart from when I'm diverted from my chosen path by a phone call from a lunatic. Or, if not a lunatic . . .

My darling husband.

"Is this one of your hilarious stunts, Alex? It doesn't sound like you, but – "

"I won't let you hurt us," the voice hisses.

"*What?*" All right, so it's not Alex. Menacing isn't his genre. Then who the hell is she and what's she talking about?

"I don't want to have to hurt you either," she says. "So why don't you pack up and go back to Muswell Hill? Then we can all stay safe."

I stumble and nearly lose my balance. Which seems unlikely, given that I thought I was standing still. Many things seem unlikely, and yet here they are in my life and kitchen.

She knows where we lived before.

Now I'm concerned. Until she said "Muswell Hill," I'd assumed her words were not meant for me.

"Please tell me your name and what you want from me," I say. "I swear on my life and everything I hold dear: I haven't a clue who you are. And I'm not prepared to have any kind of conversation with someone who won't identify herself, so . . ." I stop. The line is dead.

I KNOCK ON Ellen's door again. Walk straight in when she doesn't answer. She hasn't moved since I left her room. "Where is it?" she asks me.

"Where's what?"

"My . . . thing. For school."

"Thing? Oh." The family tree and story beginning. I took them with me when I ran to answer the phone. "I must have left them in the kitchen. Sorry. I'll bring them up in a minute." I wait, hoping she'll berate me for first reading and then removing them without permission. She says nothing.

"Shall I go and get them now?"

Er, yes? How would you like it if I took some important papers of yours and spread them all over the house in a really inconvenient way?

It's like a haunting: the constant presence in my mind of the Ellen I've lost and wish I could find. A voice in my head supplies the missing dialogue: what she would say, should be saying.

Her real-world counterpart shrugs. She doesn't ask me who was on the phone or what they wanted. I wouldn't have told her. Still, my Ellen would ask.

Who would call me and say those things? Who would imagine I must recognize their voice when I don't? I can't think of a single person. Or a reason why someone might think I want to intimidate or hurt them.

"I can't bear this, El."

"Can't bear what?"

"You, being so . . . uncommunicative. I know something's wrong."

"Oh, not this again." She lies down on her bed and pulls the pillow over her face.

"Please trust me and tell me what's the matter. You won't be in trouble, whatever it is."

"Mum, leave it. I'll be fine."

"Which means you're not fine now." I move the pillow so that I can see her.

She sits up, snatches it back.

"Are you missing London? Is that it?"

She gives me a look that tells me I'm way off the mark.

"Dad, then?"

"*Dad*? Why would I be missing Dad? He'll be back next week, won't he?"

It's as if I'm distracting her from something important by mentioning things she forgot about years ago.

She's not interested in you, or Alex.

Then who? What?

"Can I ask you about your story?" I say.

"If you must."

"Is it homework?"

"Yeah. But Mr. Goodrick couldn't remember when it had to be in, he said."

I sigh. The school here is better than the one in London in almost every way. The one exception is Ellen's form tutor, Craig Goodrick, a failed rock musician who has never managed to get my name right, though he did once get it promisingly wrong: he called me Mrs. Morrison, which isn't that far removed from Ms. Merrison. When I suggested he call me Justine, he winked and said, "Right you are, Justin," and I couldn't tell if he was deliberately winding me up or awkwardly flirting.

"And the homework was what?" I ask Ellen. "To write a story?"

She eyes me suspiciously. "Why are you so interested? I'd hardly be writing a story if I'd been told to draw a pie-chart, would I?"

Hallelujah. "I withdraw the question."

No reaction from Ellen.

Pull that in my courtroom again, I'll have you disbarred, counselor.

How could I explain to anyone who didn't know us that I'm worried about my daughter because she's stopped pretending to be an irascible American judge? They'd think I was insane.

"Does the story have to begin with a family tree?" I ask.

"No. Mum, seriously, stop interrogating me."

I think about saying, *I'm not keen on family trees. In fact, I loathe them.*

No, I'm not going to do that. It would be a bribe – "Chat to me like you used to and I'll tell you a juicy story" – and it wouldn't be fair.

Hardly juicy. A family tree on a child's bedroom wall. With the wrong family on it.

Cut.

That's one useful thing about having worked in television, at least: I have extensive experience of ruthless cutting. If I don't like a scene that's playing in my mind, I can make it disappear as quickly as an axed TV drama.

Usually.

"Where did you get those names from?" I ask Ellen. "Bascom and Sorrel Ingrey – "

"Mum! For God's sake!"

"Garnet, Urban, Allisande . . . they're so strange. And why did you use your own name? Why is there an Ellen in the Ingrey family?"

"I don't know. There just is. Stop inventing things to worry about. It's just a story."

I can hardly tell her that reading it made me feel as if I'd swallowed a lead weight. "Yes, and you've decided to put things in your story for a reason."

"I didn't think about the names." Ellen studies her fingernails, avoiding my eye. "I wanted to make the story sound old-fashioned and sinister, I suppose."

"You succeeded," I tell her. The heavy feeling in the pit of my stomach lifts a little. Maybe there's nothing to worry about after all. "You should add dates. To the family tree – not necessarily to the story. What time period are you in? What year did Perrine Ingrey murder Malachy Dodd?"

"I don't know!" Ellen snaps. "Some time in the past. And don't talk about the characters as if they're real. Ugh, it's embarrassing."

That's her. She's still in there.

"Look, it's only some stupid homework," she says, expressionless again. "It doesn't matter to anyone. Twenty years ago, twenty-five. What do dates matter? It's just a story. Why do you care?"

Am I deliberately trying to enrage her because any reaction would be better than blank withdrawal? She isn't nearly angry enough. The old Ellen would never have tolerated this level of interference or said that any creative project of hers didn't matter. By now I would have been having clothes thrown at me.

"I care, Ellen. Why did you put a murderer in your bedroom?"

"What?" For a fleeting moment, I see my own fear reflected in her eyes. Then it's gone.

"Perrine Ingrey. Her bedroom in the story is this room." I point to the little mint-green door by the side of Ellen's bed. *A quarter of the size of the shortest dwarf in the world.*

"No reason," says Ellen. "Literally, *no* reason. I needed a room, this is a room . . ." She shrugs.

"I wondered if maybe it's going to turn out that Perrine didn't kill Malachy Dodd after all. That someone else did."

"No, because it says more than once that she *did* kill him. That part's not in doubt. You can't have read it very carefully."

"I read it four times. I thought all the stuff about her killing him was protesting too much, and that – "

"*No*, Mother. That would be a cheat. It's in the third person. That wouldn't be an unreliable narrator, it would be me, the author, lying. You can't do that."

I smile. "How do you know the unreliable narrator rules? Not from Mr. Goodrick?" This is a man who regularly cancels proper lessons in favor of impromptu circle-singing sessions. I chose Ellen's school because of its unusual flexibility, then quickly realized that I didn't want it to flex for anyone but me.

A miracle happens. Ellen smiles back. "What do you think? Mr. Fisher, the Nerd King, gave us a mini-lecture about narrative perspective, including unreliable narrators. It was *so* boring. His class is doing the story homework too. All Mr. Goodrick said was 'Don't use the word "said."' He wants us to use more interesting speech words. That's why everyone in my story exclaims and yelps, in case you didn't notice."

"I didn't. I think I'd yelp if I encountered an Ingrey. And there's nothing wrong with 'said,' *said* your mother."

Too late. Ellen has shut down again. We were starting to talk properly, like we used to, so she had to distance herself.

Mr. Fisher – which one is he? The Scottish hard-blinker with the huge glasses? His first name is something Celtic-sounding. Lorgan? Lechlade?

"Why did you choose a murder mystery story?" I ask Ellen. "And why do the Ingreys have to live in our house? I'm not sure I want to share it with the weirdest family in the whole of Kingswear, even if they are fictional."

Ellen gives me an unfathomable look. "Are you thinking Perrine Ingrey's going to get murdered in my bedroom? She isn't. Don't worry. She doesn't get killed in the house or the grounds."

"Then where?"

"I haven't written it yet."

"Still. It sounds as if you know."

"I'm saying: you don't have to worry about murders in your house." Ellen rolls her eyes. "If you're so addicted to drama, go back to work, for God's sake."

"I'm not addicted to – "

"Really? Then why are you always imagining things that sound like the beginnings of really crap TV movies?"

Happily, I feel no urge to point out that nothing I made was crap. *You are dead to me, old life and former career.* I'm proud of different things these days – proud that this morning I sat on the doorstep for nearly an hour, wrapped in a blanket, watching the boats on the river.

"Like that thing with the house on the North Circular – your weird premonition," Ellen says. "I bet you never bothered to Google it, did you?"

"No. Why? Did you?"

She nods. "You were right, German isn't its name. It's Germander. You must have seen the outlines of the three missing letters. *Germander.* Do you get it now?"

"Germander Speedwell." I know the right answer, but can't immediately work out what conclusion I'm supposed to draw.

It's a plant. I hadn't heard of it until I looked up the name Speedwell, after our first tour with the real estate agent. *Veronica chamaedrys*: an herbaceous perennial plant with hairy stems and leaves. Blue four-lobed flowers. Otherwise known as Germander Speedwell.

"You saw a house called Germander and you connected it with Speedwell House because of the plant name," says Ellen. "That's why you had that weird feeling.

That and Dad being an arse and saying, 'Look, there's our new house.' It's so obvious."

"Don't call Dad an arse," I say distractedly.

Is this the resolution of a four-month-old mystery? Can I put up a big "Solved" sign in my head? It bothers me that I'm unable to answer the question definitively. I need to tell Alex, see what he thinks. Did I see the outline of the three missing letters? I don't remember seeing them.

"How long have you known?" I ask Ellen.

"Couple of months."

"Why didn't you tell me as soon as you found out?"

"I didn't know how you'd react. For all I knew, you'd start wiffling on about the name connection being even more of a sign that you were destined to live there one day."

"Yet you've told me now."

I'm glad she did, even if it doesn't cancel out the strong feeling I had.

"What made you Google that house, months after we drove past it?" I ask.

"Nothing. I don't remember. I was probably bored one day. Have you finished interrogating me now? Because it's getting old."

"Sorry." *No further questions.* "I'll go and get your story."

"No, chuck it," says Ellen. "I've already typed it up. I'm writing the rest on my laptop."

For which I know the four-digit access code.

"Don't waste your time," Ellen says with quiet efficiency. "I've password-protected the file."

LATER THAT NIGHT when she's asleep, I sit down to do the online search I probably should have done a long time ago. What did Ellen type into the Google box? "German, 8 Panama Row, London"? I try it. I didn't do it sooner because I didn't think there was any point. What could the internet tell me that would be useful? "This house is famous for provoking spooky feelings of belonging in people who have no connection with it"?

Here it is: Germander, and the correct address. I'm looking at some kind of planning application document. The owner of 8 Panama Row seems to be an Olwen Brawn, or at least that was who wanted to stick a conservatory on the side of the house in June 2012. She might have moved by now, I suppose.

A conservatory? With a lovely view of the six-lane North Circular? Evidently she decided against it or else permission wasn't granted. There was no side conservatory when I saw the house four months ago.

Olwen Brawn. The name has no effect on me at all, which is a relief.

Could Ellen be right? Was it the first six letters of Germander that did it, and Alex pointing and saying, "There's the house we've bought"? *And the heat, the stress of moving day, the traffic jam . . .*

I'd like to believe that's all it was.

The computer screen in front of me is too tempting. I go back to the Google page and type "Bascom Sorrel Ingrey Speedwell" into the search box. Nothing useful comes up, though I do find a man by the unlikely name of Bascom Sorrell, with two *l*'s, in Nicholas County, Kentucky.